STATE COLLEGE
3 3086 00396028 1

P9-CSH-226

The Storyteller's Daughter

The Storyteller's Daughter

Jean Thesman

Houghton Mifflin Company
Boston 1997

For information about this and other Houghton Mifflin trade
and reference books and multimedia products, visit
The Bookstore at Houghton Mifflin on the World Wide Web
at http://www.hmco.com/trade/.

Printed in the United States of America
The type of this book is set in 13 point Elegant Garamond.
BP 10 9 8 7 6 5 4 3 2 1

Library of Congress Cataloging-in-Publication Data
Thesman, Jean.
The storyteller's daughter / Jean Thesman.
p. cm.
Summary: Fifteen-year-old Quinn, the middle child in a
Depression-era, working class family, learns some secrets about
her beloved father, who has always been a source of strength
and optimism for his family, friends, and neighbors.
ISBN 0-395-80978-9
[1. Fathers and daughters —Fiction. 2. Depression —
1929 — Fiction. 3. Family life — Fiction.
4. City and town life — Fiction.] I. Title.
PZ7.T3525St 1997
[Fic] — dc20 96-1756 CIP AC

Also by Jean Thesman

Appointment with a Stranger
Cattail Moon
The Last April Dancers
Molly Donnelly
The Ornament Tree
Rachel Chance
The Rain Catchers
When the Road Ends

This is for the girls of Tapestry Hill,
who grew up to tell us the stories.

The Storyteller's Daughter

One

"I feel guilty, planning things without the other person knowing I'm doing it," Quinn Wagner said. Even in the dark, she felt uncomfortable enough to turn her face away.

She and her best friend, Donna Payne, sat on the stone steps that led up to the Wagners' gate. Mindful of their mothers' teachings, they kept their starched cotton skirts tucked carefully around their knees. But neither of the mothers would have approved of their conversation.

"Sometimes boys are so thick-headed that you *have* to plan things," Donna said.

"You can't see into Justin's bedroom window, can you?" Quinn asked, lowering her voice.

"No, of course not, but I can see his light from our kitchen window. Why didn't you say something encouraging to him when he got here tonight?"

"You mean like, 'Justin, will you go to the community center dance with me?'" Quinn sighed. "How could I do that? I didn't even dare say hello. We were eating dinner on the porch, and if I'd said a single word to him out there in front of everybody, Feep would never let me forget it. Anyway, Justin got out of his dad's car on the other side of the street and maybe he wouldn't have heard me, unless I yelled. Feep would really have loved that."

"Sometimes I don't like your brother," Donna said seriously.

"I know what you mean," Quinn acknowledged. "He's a terrible pest. Listen, do you hear a car?"

Both girls held their breaths in the dark and strained to hear the sound they waited for.

"I think it turned off somewhere," Donna said finally. "Your dad's late tonight, isn't he?"

"It can't be more than nine-thirty," Quinn said. "That's not so late. But he missed his favorite radio program."

John Wagner, who was called Beau John by his family and friends, and even by the enemy who would betray him, had lost his job as a bookkeeper early in 1933. Months later, when he found work again, it was as a dock laborer in a resort town far to the north of Seattle where passenger boats unloaded vacationers and cargo. He only came home on Saturday nights, stayed twenty-four hours, and then he left again. This arrangement was hard on him and his family, but even the children knew that finding any job during the Depression was a miracle, and he had many people to support.

"Things will be different this August," Donna said, returning to their favorite subject, young Justin Dallas, nephew of the elderly Dallas sisters who lived across Farrow Street, the gravel side road. "You'll be working for Miss Clotilde, and Justin will be in and out of the cottage all day long."

"But if he didn't notice me last summer, why would he notice me this summer?" Quinn asked. "He lives on the other side of Seattle, so he could have a special girlfriend and I wouldn't know." Automatically, her fingers went to her long, dark braid, and she retied the blue plaid ribbon on the end of it.

"He'll notice you now because now you're fifteen and he's fifteen, and everybody notices everybody when they're that old."

"Here comes another car," Quinn interrupted.

They listened as the car drew closer. When it passed under a streetlight, Quinn recognized it.

"Beau John's home," she said, and her voice broke with relief.

The car stopped in front of the Wagner house, and Quinn's father got out. The girls jumped up to greet him, and he bent to kiss Quinn's forehead and rumple Donna's curly red hair.

"Ladies, what are you doing out here in the dark?" Beau John asked.

"It's too hot to stay inside," Quinn told him. "Anyway, the family's playing cards and hollering again."

Beau John laughed and shook his head. "Daughter, you know the arguing is only in fun. What's a card game without a little yelling?"

"It's only fun if you're out of earshot, Beau John," Quinn complained.

"Who's winning?" her father asked.

"Who else but Grandma?" Quinn said.

"I should go home now," Donna said. "The mosquitoes are eating me up. Everybody will be glad you're back again, Beau John. Dad says he keeps forgetting you're away and watches for you strolling up and down the block after dinner."

"Tell him I'll be looking him up," Beau John said. "Go on and get out of reach of those mosquitoes, Donna. We'll hear you through your gate." He meant that he and Quinn would wait out on the sidewalk until she had crossed Farrow Street, run around the corner to Maple Road past the Dallas sisters' cottage, and turned into her own gate. It was a courtesy. No one worried about safety in that neighborhood.

"Good night, then," Donna called as she hurried out of sight in the dark. They heard her shoes click on the sidewalk on Maple Road, and then her gate slammed behind her.

"Now let's go in and break up the riot," Beau John said.

They could hear Feep arguing shrilly as they climbed the stone steps and pushed through the old wooden gate. Ahead, light spilled out of the windows and the screen door and illuminated the broad porch that ran around two sides of the large, shabby house.

"How's everyone been since I left?" Beau John asked his daughter as he took the porch steps two at a time.

"Uncle Dick's over his cold and Mama's been feeling pretty good," Quinn had time to say before Beau John opened the screen door.

"Beau John!" nine-year-old Phillip screamed when he saw his father.

Everyone else looked up. "You should have been here, brother," Uncle Dick declared. "These women are beating me at every game."

"It's because Gammie cheats!" Feep cried. "Beau John! She's *your* mother. Make her quit!"

"I can cheat if I want to," Grandma said crossly, tossing her curly white hair while she shuffled cards. "It's a privilege of old age."

"That's right, Feep," Amy said. Quinn's seventeen-year-old sister got to her feet and hugged her father. "Grandma gets to do anything she wants, doesn't she? Feep knows the rules. Did you have a good week, Beau John? Are you tired?"

"I'm fit as ever, thank you." Beau John bent over his wife, who raised her thin face for his kiss. "Nancy, do you suppose one of you ladies could make me a sandwich? I missed dinner."

Mrs. Wagner jumped up. "You drove all this way on an empty stomach?" she cried.

"No, no, I used the car, not my empty stomach," Beau John said, and everyone, even Feep, laughed.

"Do you want coffee, too?" Auntie Sis asked over her shoulder as she followed Quinn's mother from the room.

"Coffee sounds good," Beau John declared. He shook the hand that his brother held out to him. "Quinn says you're better, Dick. I believe you have more color in your face."

"I'm fine, fine," Uncle Dick said. "And Nancy's been getting along better than usual. Amy found a new kind of medicine for her trouble, some tablets she can buy without a prescription."

Beau John smiled at his elder daughter. "Did you, dearie?"

"It was only a lucky chance," Amy said, her heart-shaped face turning pink. "There's a drugstore on the first floor of the building where I work, and the pharmacist is a nice man, so I told him about Mama's rheumatic heart."

The family was proud of Amy, and Quinn could never decide if she envied her or not. Amy had quit high school after her junior year and found an office job a few weeks later. She earned two dollars for each ten-hour day, and worked five and a half days every week, but even that small amount of money was a blessing for her family.

Uncle Dick and Auntie Sis had moved in the year before, after they lost their jobs and their house. Grandma had joined the household earlier, after the bank where she kept her small savings closed its doors against its customers and never opened them again.

All the money anyone in the household earned went into the cigar box Mama hid in the pantry behind the jars of crabapple jelly. Most of the time they considered themselves lucky.

Grandma followed the other women to the kitchen to help fix a meal for Beau John. Uncle Dick cleared the cards off the round oak table in the middle of the parlor, snapped a rubber band around the deck, and put it away on a bookcase shelf.

"Eat in here with us," he said. "I got that radio working again, Beau John, but I don't believe there'd be anything on the air this late. Do you want me to try?"

Beau John raised a hand in protest. "No, no, Dick. But I'll count on you to keep me company tomorrow when Jack Benny is on the air."

"Beau John, tell us what happened on the dock this week," Quinn asked. She slid into her usual chair, between Feep and Amy.

Beau John pulled out his chair and sat down, too.

"You won't believe what I saw yesterday," he said. "There was a man sitting on the rail of a ship and playing a flute. That would be a strange sight, at the dock where the toughs hang out. But he had a dancing dog with him, a little black-and-white fellow with a tail like a plume, and it reminded me of the dog I had when I was a boy . . ."

"Ming Toy," Quinn supplied. She had heard of his dog before.

"Ming Toy, yes," Beau John said. "She was another dancing dog, the best of them all. They say the dancing ones understand every word we say, no matter what language we speak."

Everyone believed him. Everyone always believed him. Quinn, smiling, listened to the rest of his story, and she was filled with pride. Handsome, gentle Beau John was a thoroughly good man, well-known all over the Tapestry Hill neighborhood for his kindness and for his stories.

"He could be on the radio," Miss Clotilde Dallas had told Quinn once.

"He could be in the moving pictures," her sister, Miss Ramona said.

Quinn was certain they were right.

Feep was allowed to stay up until his father finished eating, but everyone agreed that it would be a terrible mistake ever to allow the boy that particular favor again, since he whined and kicked a table leg all through the meal. Grandma had to drag him out of the parlor while he screamed, "Daddy, make her stop!" Feep was the only one in the family who dropped Beau John's affectionate nickname when he was upset.

"He's worse than ever," Amy said disgustedly.

Beau John shook his head. "That's my fault, for being away so much. Sooner or later I'll find something in Seattle. I'm sure of it. Hard times never last forever."

"It's *my* fault Feep's such a brat," Mama said.

"Don't let me hear you say that," Auntie Sis said quickly. "It was a heart-scald for you when Feep's twin died, and only six months old, too."

Uncle Dick cleared his throat and pulled out his old silver pocket watch, winding it while he talked. "Big day tomorrow, Beau John. The ladies have a picnic planned."

"Now isn't that something to look forward to," Beau John said with great satisfaction. "I hope we're going up to the meadow. I heard there'll be maybe twenty planes at the airfield tomorrow, and stunt flying and even some skywriting."

"The whole neighborhood's climbing the hill tomorrow," Auntie Sis said, nodding with satisfaction. She loved neighborhood gatherings of any kind, even funerals.

Later, after everyone else had gone upstairs, Quinn could hear Auntie Sis clearing the table. She would turn out the lights, checking each room twice the way she always did. The night was still uncomfortably hot, so she would leave the front and back doors standing open.

Quinn and Amy shared the front bedroom that overlooked Maple Road. To Quinn, there didn't seem to be enough air in the room, so after Amy fell asleep, she got out of bed and pushed their window open even farther.

She saw headlights moving down Maple Road, but heard nothing. It had to be Mike O'Hara, sneaking Betty Caster home again. When he brought her back this late, he turned off the engine and coasted down the hill.

Mike was twenty-two, and he actually owned a car! It was easy to believe the neighborhood rumors that he worked for his gangster uncle.

Well, Betty wouldn't care. She, like Amy, had quit high school early, but Betty worked as an usherette at the neighborhood theater across the bridge from Tapestry Hill, spent all her money on clothes, and bragged that Mike had promised to buy her a house when they got married.

Quinn yanked the shade down again and returned to bed.

"What?" Amy asked sleepily from her bed. "Who?"

"You sound like an owl," Quinn said. "Go back to sleep."

Faintly, both girls heard Betty's stifled laughter through the open window.

"Her again," Amy said disgustedly. She turned over in bed and kicked off the sheet that covered her. "I can't stand her. When she washes handkerchiefs — *when* she washes them — she plasters them to her window pane and lets them dry there so she doesn't have to iron them. She does that with her hair ribbons, too. And those satin uniforms she wears at the theater are dirty. The collars are absolutely grimy."

"I'm going downstairs to sleep on the sofa if you don't stop talking about her dirty clothes," Quinn said. "She and Mike both make me gag."

"I know," Amy said, yawning hugely. "They're awful. But he's got a new car, and Beau John keeps ours running by praying over it."

"Uncle Dick's car runs just fine."

"Ha," Amy said. "Someday he'll find another carpenter's job and they'll move away and take the car with them."

After a while, Quinn heard Mike's tires roll over gravel as he coasted down the rest of the hill. A moment later, she heard an engine start in the distance.

The bedroom was stifling. Quinn got up again and padded downstairs in her bare feet, heading for the kitchen and a glass of cold water from the electric refrigerator Uncle Dick and Auntie Sis had brought with them when they moved in. She hadn't turned on the lights, but she could see well enough to find her way.

She was halfway across the kitchen, when she heard soft voices outside the door. For a moment, she was startled, but then she crept across the floor to listen. Who was out there on their porch at this time of night? It must have been after midnight.

". . . told you before I didn't want any part of it," she heard Beau John say.

"And I told you that you don't have a choice," another man said. He sounded older than Beau John. Rougher. "Doubling the shipment means more money for everybody. That could mean a lot to your family, at least for as long as the game lasts. But get this straight — you're either all the way in or all the way out, and if you're out, don't bother starting up your car tomorrow. I came here tonight for your answer, just like I said. What's it to be, Beau John?"

Two

What was going on out there in the dark? Who was that man who spoke so rudely to her father? Quinn took an impulsive step forward, then stopped. Caution — and fear — got the better of her.

Beau John still hadn't answered the man.

"It's that or nothing," the man said. "In times like these, we can find a dozen men to replace you. The minute the law changes we'll all be out of business, so grab the money while you can."

Quinn heard her father sigh. Then he said, "All right. But it'll mean jail for all of us if we're caught. A little risk is one thing. Spitting in the face of the Federal boys — and that's what you're doing by doubling the loads — that's asking for trouble. The law hasn't changed yet. Don't count on what you don't have."

"It won't be the Federal boys," the man said. "How many times do I have to tell you that? There aren't enough of them to go around, and they don't bother with us small fry, not unless somebody does most of the work for them. If anything goes wrong, you'll be dealing with the county boys, and you'll always carry enough cash to handle them on the spot."

"Driving a big load like that will attract hijackers. We might get away into a side road with the small truck, but there's no hiding a big one."

"Worst comes to worst, you can hand over the truck and walk away. Saving the load's not your problem. Is it a done deal, Beau John? I don't want to waste any more time here listening to you fret yourself into a fiddle string."

"You don't leave me a choice," Beau John said. "But don't come back to my house again. I don't like it."

"Take it easy, take it easy," the man said. He left silently, disappearing into the dark.

Quinn ducked down behind the kitchen table just as her father walked through the door. He shut it, paused a moment to look through the window into the night, sighed, and moved quietly toward the hall.

Quinn left her hiding place only when she heard the stairs creak under his weight.

Once Beau John had told Quinn a story about a princess who eavesdropped. Each word the princess overheard turned into a stone that she had to carry in a bag. The bag grew heavier and heavier, but she wouldn't stop snooping. Finally the bag was so heavy that it caused her to topple over the castle wall, and she drowned in the moat, still holding on to the bag.

What Quinn overheard in those few moments was a greater burden to her than any bag of stones.

She didn't sleep much that night. Once she almost woke her sister, to tell her what she'd overheard. But she wanted the man at their back door to be a figure in a nightmare and the conversation nothing more than her imagination. No one must ever find out about the stranger — and the kind of work Beau John had been doing. By morning she had done her best to convince herself that she had dreamed about the visitor.

At breakfast, while Grandma filled her cup from the teapot, the old woman said without warning, "I like that young Justin. He's a hard worker and he doesn't sass his elders."

Quinn could have added to the list of Justin's virtues, but even on a happier day she would have kept her opinion to herself on this particular subject. The family didn't know about her fascination with the boy who stayed in their neighborhood every August.

"It's nice of him to help his aunts bring in their peaches," Auntie Sis said. "Poor Mr. Shadwell isn't good for much of anything these days."

Mr. Shadwell was a mysterious, ragged old man who had lived in a shed at the back of the Dallas sisters' orchard for all of Quinn's life at least. No one ever heard him speak. Before arthritis crippled him almost completely, he busied himself with light chores for Miss Clotilde and Miss Ramona, but now he could do little except rake the cinder path that ran along the edge of Farrow Street.

"Donna says they pay Justin plenty, so he's really working for them, not just helping out," Quinn said, giving in to the spiteful impulse to make Justin at least a little less than perfect, now that Beau John's feet seemed to be made of clay.

Beau John was a smuggler? A rumrunner?

What had her father been doing out there in the dark with a stranger? What was that talk about trucks and "Federal boys" and hijackers?

Why couldn't she think about something else!

Feep looked up from under his shaggy blond hair. "If Justin goes up to the meadow to watch the air show, he and Quinn can sneak off into the woods and go kiss-kiss-kiss." He kissed the back of his hand noisily several times to emphasize his point.

"Mama!" Quinn cried, horrified. She blushed so hard that even her ears burned.

"Oh, Phillip, for heaven's sake," Mama protested. "Leave your sister alone — and get over here to the sink. You've got jelly all over your face. And what did you do to your shirt? It's missing most of its buttons. You look like an orphan."

"Orphans don't eat jelly," Feep grumbled. "My library book says they eat gruel. What's gruel? Is that what Mr. Shadwell eats out of that old tin bowl because he doesn't have any teeth?"

"Oh, mercy," Mama groaned, rolling her eyes. She snatched a wet washrag from the edge of the sink and scrubbed Feep's face harder than necessary, until he bellowed for help.

"Don't call *me* for help, whatever you do," Uncle Dick said, and he shot Feep a long look. "Mr. Shadwell told me you've been up on our roof again."

Feep pulled free from his mother. "He can't talk!" he cried. "He can't tell you anything."

"He went like this," Uncle Dick said, and he flapped his arms. "He looked like a crazy, squawking chicken going 'Feep! Feep! Feep!' — and he pointed to our roof. I knew exactly what he meant."

Feep charged for the hall door, and turned back to shout, "When I'm a famous airplane pilot, you'll be sorry you made fun of me."

"He didn't take an umbrella up on the roof again, did he?" Mama asked, horrified. Earlier in the summer, Feep had jumped from the porch roof with an open umbrella, a substitute for a parachute. His hard landing damaged only the umbrella, but it had frightened his family to a degree that satisfied him immensely.

"Mr. Shadwell shook his head 'no' when I asked him," Uncle Dick said. He laughed a little. "Then he did this." He held up his crossed index fingers. "I think he believes Feep is possessed."

"Well, that's better than crazy old Elizabetta De-Piano's sign warding off the evil eye," Grandma said as she stirred extra sugar into her tea with more energy than necessary. "I hate it when she does that to me."

"She does that to everybody," Auntie Sis said. "I told you before not to take it seriously."

"I take it seriously because she must have said something to her priest about me. When I passed him on the old Graham Street bridge, he crossed himself."

"Everybody makes all kinds of signs when they walk across that wreck," Auntie Sis said. "Before I start out on it, I spit three times over the railing."

"I'm sure the men down below in Hooverville appreciate that," Beau John said, his bright blue eyes watching her over the edge of his coffee cup.

Everyone laughed, even Quinn, who hadn't been sure she'd ever laugh again.

Nothing was wrong. What she had heard the night before was what eavesdroppers always heard, bits and pieces that don't make sense. She wished she hadn't stayed to listen, but that couldn't be helped. She could only try to put the conversation out of her mind.

Of course nothing was wrong. Beau John was — Beau John.

By eleven o'clock, the Wagners and half the neighborhood had gathered on the rocky meadow that crowned

Tapestry Hill. They had a perfect view of the flying field with its yellow and red private planes and its row of hangars. A commercial passenger plane sat at the end of the field. On Monday, a dozen lucky people with important business in San Francisco would board it for the first leg of its journey south.

The women spread blankets on the dry yellow grass. The men, smoking pipes or hand-rolled cigarettes, gathered at the edge of the meadow and watched the activities at the flying field where other men made mysterious trips in and out of the hangars. The young people stayed with the men and listened to their talk of airplanes.

"Before long passenger planes will be coming and going every day from Seattle," one man said.

"I'll believe it when I see it," another said. "Who needs to go anywhere that fast? It's not natural."

Justin, who had carried the Dallas sisters' picnic basket up the hill, stood with the boys and watched the planes. Donna nudged Quinn and looked sideways at him.

"Have you talked to him yet?" Donna whispered.

Quinn shook her head. "They were ahead of us on the path, but he didn't notice me."

"Oh, he noticed you," Donna said loyally. "Sure he did."

But Justin wasn't so important to Quinn any longer.

She had waited all year for his annual visit to his aunts, imagining all sorts of delightful possibilities involving the summer dance at the community center, evenings at the movies, and visits to the ice-cream parlor across the street from the theater. Now her attention was fixed on her father.

Beau John was respected by everyone. She saw how the other men sought out his opinions, how they laughed at his stories. Crippled Mr. Shadwell, struggling up the steep path after everyone else, touched Beau John's arm to get his attention, and smiled with his lips shut tight.

"Mr. Shadwell, I got good use out of that wrench you let me borrow last week," Beau John said. He patted the old man's shoulder. "On my own, I'd never have thought of using it the way you showed me."

Mr. Shadwell's eyes sparkled and he nodded. He seemed to stand a little taller. Perhaps he even seemed younger. Beau John had that effect on people. Reflected in his eyes, they saw themselves differently — better and smarter — and they loved Beau John for it.

But then two men began discussing the front page news in the Sunday papers. Smugglers had been seen unloading crates of whiskey south of Seattle on a Puget Sound beach. No one had been caught, but the police assured the community that they would remain alert.

"Alert with their palms out," one man said, laughing.

Beau John smoked and watched the airfield, and he said nothing.

After a while, the women called the men and children to lunch. Donna sat close enough to Quinn to talk to her throughout the meal. Their mothers, old friends, discussed the absence of Betty Caster and her mother in lowered voices.

"Lizzie Caster's gone back to the Catholic church," Mrs. Payne murmured. "I don't have a thing against Catholics, but Father Sully gets crazier every year, and he won't let anybody in his church socialize with Protestants."

"Except for Lizzie, the DePianos never had anything to do with the rest of us," Mama said. "They always did keep to the other Catholics, even before Father Sully came. But they weren't rude then."

"Lucky us," Mrs. Payne murmured, laughing. "But Lizzie Caster's always been a real friendly woman, and I was shocked when she told me she wouldn't come today because her brother and his family wouldn't. Heavens above, Nancy. Wouldn't you think this meadow was big enough for all of us?"

"It's because of Betty," Mama said. "Her mother wants somebody to help her get Betty away from that Mike. He's not Catholic Irish. His people were Orangemen. Sooner or later, Father Sully will run Mike off, you can be sure of that. He hates Protestants and gangsters."

"Don't forget Communists," Grandma said. "I heard

tell that he's got the phone number of the F.B.I., and if you know a Communist — or even a rumrunner — he'll call the government people for you."

"Sakes," Mama said disgustedly. "But it would be better if Betty stopped seeing that Mike, and if the priest can help, I suppose it's all right."

"Mama," Amy said, leaning forward over her plate. "Betty doesn't go to church anyway, so nothing Father Sully says will make any difference."

Since Amy quit school and went to work, the women in the neighborhood moved over and made room for her among themselves. She was no longer considered a child, and her opinions were shown respect.

"That's true enough, Amy," Mrs. Payne said. "Well, this will make an interesting mess."

The air show began when two yellow biplanes took off at the same time and crossed over the field, trailing blue smoke. Conversation died down while the daring pilots' loops and spins brought shrieks from the crowd below.

Quinn watched, but her thoughts were somewhere else. Betty's Mike was a gangster. Everyone knew that gangsters were responsible for liquor being brought into the country from Canada. Movies had been made about smugglers and rumrunners. The newspapers were full of their exploits. But the new president, Franklin Roosevelt, was determined to end Prohibition, and when that happened, selling liquor would be legal again. Mike would have to find a new job. He might be more acceptable to Betty's mother then.

And Beau John? Was he mixed up in this somehow? But Quinn felt like a traitor, even wondering about it.

She glanced over at her father, who was offering a bowl of cold fried chicken to Mr. Shadwell. "We have plenty," he said. "We can't eat it all ourselves. See if the ladies want a little more."

He meant the Dallas sisters, who sat on a log under a madrona tree at the edge of the woods. They were deep in conversation with Mrs. Bonner, whose husband had been killed the year before when the impoverished veterans of the Great War had marched on Washington, demanding the bonuses they had been promised for serving their country. Mrs. Bonner's little boy, James Aaron, never played with the other neighborhood children. They lived in a house even smaller than the Dallas's cottage, and they would have to leave it soon. The bank was taking it away from Mrs. Bonner because she couldn't pay her mortgage.

Beau John and Mama took food to Mrs. Bonner sometimes.

There was no way Beau John could be a criminal.

After the air show, everyone wandered back down the hill to their shaded yards. Grandma and Auntie Sis served watermelon to the family on the side porch, in the shade of the tallest maple tree in the neighborhood. Across the gravel side street, Justin moved among the peach trees, picking fruit. Quinn caught occasional glimpses of his light blue shirt. Up Maple Road, in the Paynes' front yard, a sprinkler whirled and hissed.

After a while Beau John napped in the hammock slung between two trees in the back yard until Uncle Dick woke him when Jack Benny came on the radio. Mama and Grandma began preparations for a dinner of leftover salad, sliced ham, and a cobbler made from the peaches the Dallas sisters had given Grandma the day before.

Amy had washed her hair as soon as they returned from the picnic and had wound it in curling rags to dry while they waited for dinner. She sat next to Quinn on the porch steps and filed her nails.

"I wish we had a telephone," Amy said suddenly.

"Who would you call?" Quinn asked, amazed. "We don't know anybody with a telephone."

"Maybe somebody would call me," Amy said.

"Who?" Quinn asked.

Amy laughed. "Now *you* sound like an owl."

"But who would call you?" Quinn asked.

Amy shrugged, but she was blushing.

"A boy?" Quinn asked. "Amy, what would Mama say?"

"I'm seventeen," Amy said. "Somebody could call me if he wanted to."

Quinn didn't want to go on with the conversation. The idea that Amy might attract serious attention from someone was too disturbing. It was all right to daydream about Justin and wonder what it might be like to sit next to him in a dark theater. It was quite different to have someone use the telephone and ask . . . what? What would this boy ask Amy? For a real date?

"Beau John wouldn't like it," Quinn said crossly. "Why don't you put your hair up in pincurls instead of using curling rags?"

"Why don't you curl your hair with anything you like?" Amy asked. "Your braid is too old-fashioned."

Quinn blinked. "How come you're crabby?"

Amy sighed. "I don't know. Sometimes I think about Betty, with all her clothes and her hope chest full of dish towels and sheets, and Mike dying to marry her, and I wonder what's going to happen to me?"

"Something better than what's going to happen to Betty, I hope," Quinn said.

Amy threw her arms around Quinn. "That's what I love about you. You're so logical, like Mama. Not anything like Beau John."

The family ate dinner on the porch, and afterward Beau John told his family goodbye and climbed back into his dusty car.

"I'll see you next Saturday," he called out to them.

Quinn pressed both hands to her mouth to keep from crying out, "Beau John, please! Don't go." Her family would think she was crazy!

She watched her father's car labor up the street and out of sight, and she knew suddenly, and with a terrible certainty, that she would not be seeing him next Saturday.

Across the side street, Mr. Shadwell stepped out on the cinder path with his rake. He and Quinn stared at each other for a long moment, and then Mr. Shadwell shook his head sadly and began his slow raking.

He felt it, Quinn thought. That awful cold fear touched him, too. He knows Beau John is in trouble.

Three

Quinn was late to the breakfast table Monday morning. She had spent most of the night staring at the bedroom ceiling, and after she fell asleep at dawn, her sleep was wracked with bad dreams and didn't last long. When she got up and went downstairs in her bathrobe, she found Amy ready to leave for work.

"You look so nice," Quinn told her. "I can't get over how grown-up you seem in your office dress."

Amy, yanking on neat white gloves, said, "Mama wants me to put aside money for a winter dress. When I have enough, I hope you'll go shopping with me."

"Heavens, we'll all go," Auntie Sis said. "If you'll let us, that is."

"And we'll have lunch in that nice cafeteria in the basement of the Triangle Building," Mama said. "A new office dress is worth a celebration."

"You're leaving me out?" Uncle Dick asked, pretending great offense. "You ladies are going downtown for doodads and lunch, and leaving me out?"

"Dick, you know you'd hate it," Auntie Sis said.

"Men don't belong at lunch with the ladies," Grandma said briskly as she filled a plate with hotcakes and bacon for Quinn. "They're too loud."

Quinn expected Feep to holler up a storm because it was obvious he'd be left out of the shopping trip, but he didn't look up from his plate, and before Quinn had buttered her toast, Feep jumped up from the table and ran to the back door.

" 'Scuse me," he said, and he was gone.

"Where's he going?" Quinn asked her mother.

"To Monkey's. They've got some sort of project going out back of the woodshed. Mercy, I wish he'd find another best friend. Somebody more polite and dependable than that scamp, Monkey. Does anybody want more coffee?"

"I want coffee, please," Quinn said boldly.

"When you're sixteen," Mama said automatically. "Are you feeling all right, Quinn? You look pale."

"I'm fine, Mama," Quinn said.

"Another pancake?" Grandma said. "More bacon?"

"No, thanks," Quinn said. "Miss Clotilde expects me at nine."

Miss Clotilde Dallas had taught Quinn calligraphy the winter before, and Quinn had practiced earnestly until her lettering was beautiful. Now Miss Clotilde paid Quinn to help her when she received a large order for place cards or party invitations for the customers of the stationery department in the most elegant department store in Seattle. Quinn and Miss Clotilde had to letter three hundred place cards for a grand dinner party being given at a hotel next Saturday evening.

"We'll be envying you, sitting out there under her trees while we're down in the basement doing the laundry," Auntie Sis said.

"I'll have writer's cramp by the time you hang out the sheets," Quinn said as she folded her napkin and pushed back her chair.

"You'll certainly have it before Miss Ramona gets their sheets out," Grandma said, laughing.

Everybody knew that the Dallas sisters were always the last women in the neighborhood to hang out their wash. With Miss Clotilde busy with her calligraphy, the tail end of their wash might not go out until Tuesday.

That was all right with Quinn. She didn't want to be around when they hung out their ancient embroidered corset covers and tattered bloomers. They didn't dry their underwear inside pillow cases the way the other ladies did. And they didn't have a proper drying yard, either. Instead, their clotheslines were stretched from tree to tree in their orchard, like a web spun by a staggering, drunken spider, and in full view of God — and Justin — too.

She hurried upstairs to dress. Usually she looked forward to working with Miss Clotilde, but she was jittery and tense that morning. Two days before, she had nothing to worry about. Well, sometimes she worried about Mama's health. Now she couldn't stop the chatter in her mind.

She made her bed before she left the bedroom, and carried the laundry bag she shared with Amy downstairs for Mama to sort.

"I'll be back for lunch, unless they invite me to eat with them," she told the women in the kitchen.

When she crossed Farrow Street, she saw Justin walking through the tall dry grass in the orchard. In one hand he carried a long pole with a hook on the end of it. In the other hand, he held a wicker basket. The air was filled with the sweet scent of ripening peaches.

He looked over his shoulder when the gate latch clicked.

"Hey, Quinn," he said, with an ease she envied.

"Hey," she answered hoarsely.

Say something, she ordered herself. They were alone, for the moment, at least. This was the opportunity she and Donna had talked about for weeks. Tell Justin about the dance, she thought. Ask him if he's going to the movies Wednesday night when they have the drawing for groceries and dishes. Everybody goes, and perhaps he might sit next to her.

Ask him anything!

But her mind had gone blank. The dance, grocery night — those things didn't matter anymore. Beau John was in some kind of trouble.

Justin disappeared around the side of the house

while she struggled with her feelings, and the moment was lost.

She saw that Miss Clotilde had already spread a paper cover over the table under the crabapple tree and brought out her bottles of India ink and several small cardboard boxes of stiff blank cards.

The old woman pushed open the screen door. She was not even five feet tall, and so thin that her ink-stained fingers looked like bird claws. She had attempted to restrain her gray hair in a bun, but wiry strands straggled over her high collar. She and her sister were the only women Quinn knew who had pierced ears and wore earrings all the time. That day, Miss Clotilde wore small emeralds set in delicate gold petals. Quinn could hardly imagine any future that could include emerald earrings for herself. Neighborhood gossip about the sisters wove a complicated tale of a wealthy father, dead many years, and an unscrupulous fiancé who stole their inheritance and vanished.

Gossip, Beau John always said, was sometimes half true and half wishful thinking on everybody's part. The girls in the neighborhood agreed that a vanished fiancé was better than none at all.

"Quinn!" Miss Clotilde cried when she saw the girl. "We've got our work cut out for us this morning." She held open the screen door for Quinn, and two flies took immediate advantage, but she didn't notice. She never did.

The little kitchen was already hot, and cluttered with the bits and pieces of the sisters' hobbies and interests. Quinn helped Miss Clotilde gather up a scattering of spare pen points, almost lost among the newspapers and piano music stacked on the table. Miss Ramona gave piano lessons twice a week at the downtown music school.

Miss Ramona, sitting in a rocking chair near the window and reading sheet music as if it were simple English, glanced up at them through her thick glasses. Her hair was braided. Her earrings that day were made of small rubies surrounded by diamond chips.

"Quinn, listen to this and see if you recognize it," she said. She hummed a few bars of the music she held.

"'Mad About the Boy,'" Quinn said promptly. It was her favorite song that summer.

"I can't fool you, dearie," Miss Ramona said.

Quinn and Miss Clotilde carried their supplies outside and began work. On each card, Quinn drew a faint pencil line with a ruler. Then she dipped a pen in India ink, held her breath, and watched the first letter flow out from the nib. The customer wanted Irish uncials, her favorite letters, so she smiled as she worked.

By noon, they had lettered a full box of place cards, and they stopped to rub their aching hands and sip the lemonade Miss Ramona brought them.

"We hope you'll have lunch with us," Miss Ramona

told Quinn. "I'll call Justin and Mr. Shadwell, and we can get started."

Quinn eyed the laundry Miss Ramona had hung out that morning, and resigned herself. To reach the porch, Justin would have to weave his way past a line with a pale yellow petticoat that drooped beside a matching chemise, both dangling ragged lace and strings of narrow, shabby ribbon, and another line with long black stockings and a black satin waist-cincher, the kind called a Merry Widow. Miss Ramona had been busy in the cottage basement.

"That's very nice of you," she said. "I'd like to have lunch with you."

"We remembered how much you and Justin enjoyed tuna fish and sweet pickle sandwiches," Miss Ramona said. "So I made enough for an army."

The table under the tree was cluttered with bottles of ink, pens, and blank cards, so they went inside to the hot kitchen and used the table there. Mr. Shadwell appeared silently, washed his gnarled hands at the sink, and sat at one end of the table. He bobbed his head when Quinn said hello.

Through the window, she caught a glimpse of Justin floundering through the thicket of drying laundry, pushing bloomers and stockings out of his way, heading toward the porch. Quinn wished she could put off until tomorrow a face-to-face meeting with the boy she had spent the winter daydreaming about, but he came in, letting the screen door slam behind him, and greeted her with a broad smile.

"Hey, I'm starved," he said, eyeing the platter of sandwiches appreciatively.

He, too, washed at the sink and rubbed his hands dry on the scrap of towel hanging from a nail next to the drainboard. He sat beside Quinn and grinned at her.

"You've got ink on your chin," he said.

His hair was as blond as Beau John's, but his eyes were gray, not blue, and he had a dimple. Quinn looked away, speechless with delight.

Midway through the afternoon, Miss Clotilde complained of eyestrain, and the work stopped for the day. Quinn went next door to Donna's house, looking for a few minutes of distraction. She didn't want to go home yet, with nothing to do but think about Beau John. Maybe Donna would like to walk over the bridge to the shops and look at magazines in the drugstore.

She found her friend shelling peas in the kitchen, and nearly finished with the chore.

"She can go with you," Mrs. Payne said, "if you girls will stop by the grocery store for me on the way back."

"I'll see if Mama needs something, too," Quinn said, feeling suddenly justified in the walk since grocery shopping was certainly a good reason to stay away from home.

Both girls carried small lists and coin purses when they finally left. Half a block from home, Donna sighed and then giggled.

"I've got a surprise," she said. "I earned ten cents picking all the stitches out of Aunt Belle's old winter coat. Should we buy candy bars or a movie magazine?"

"I choose the magazine," Quinn said without hesitation because she knew that would be her friend's choice. "What's going to happen to the material from the coat?"

"Mama's making a jacket out of it," Donna said. "Did you get to talk to Justin today?"

Quinn shook her head. "Not much. The ladies were always there."

"They'll go to the movies Wednesday night," Donna said. "They always do, and I'll bet he goes with them. We'll ask him to sit with us."

Quinn laughed bitterly. "Oh, certainly. And then Peep will want to sit with us, too, and I'd rather stay home."

Donna sighed. "I *really* don't like your brother."

"You told me already," Quinn said.

Both girls began laughing, and they were still laughing when they stepped out on the infamous wooden bridge that crossed over the railroad tracks and Hooverville, the village made up of weathered packing crates and tents, where dozens of homeless men lived.

"I don't know what scares me most," Donna said. "I

hate the way the bridge creaks when we walk on it. But I hate being this close to Hooverville, too."

"I always think about that awful fairy tale when I walk over a bridge," Quinn said. "This one seems like it could really have a troll living under it. Not in Hooverville, of course — Beau John said they're mostly nice men who've had bad luck. But almost anything could be hiding behind those rocks and bushes over there on the other side."

"Oh, look!" Donna said suddenly. "Here comes crazy old Elizabetta DePiano."

Ahead of them, a woman no taller than Feep scuttled toward them. She wore a bulky black dress that touched the ground, and in spite of the heat, a thick black shawl covered her head. She carried shopping bags in both hands. As she drew closer to the girls, her wrinkled, brown-spotted face twisted into a terrible scowl. While they watched, she switched one shopping bag to the other hand and made a curious gesture toward them, with her middle fingers curled over her palm and under her thumb, and her index and little fingers pointing down.

Quinn blurted out nervous laughter. Next to her, Donna giggled helplessly.

The old woman shrieked unintelligibly and then, suddenly, she made a crude gesture that they both recognized. They responded with shocked laughter that was nearly hysterical. The old woman hobbled by, close enough for Quinn to see the long black hairs that grew on her upper lip.

Quinn and Donna were incapable of walking on. They clung to each other, howling with laughter.

"Do we have a curse on us?" Donna asked.

"I don't think that's what that last gesture means," Quinn gasped.

The old woman stopped and turned back to face them. "*Bo Zhan, I feex heem!*" she cried, and then she scrabbled across to the far side of the bridge.

"What did she say?" Donna asked. "Was it something about your dad?"

Goosebumps sprang up on Quinn's arms. "I don't think so," she said warily.

"It sounded something like 'Beau John,'" Donna said.

"She's crazy," Quinn said. "She barely knows my dad."

No cloud covered the sun, but the day seemed to have gone cold. "Let's hurry to the drugstore," Quinn said. "I'm dying to see the magazines."

Their shoes clattered on the wooden bridge as they ran to the other side, and Quinn was sure she felt the old timbers shift a little. But it was safe. Beau John promised her that it was really safe, and he never lied to her.

But he had! He had! He had said he was a dock worker, not someone whose job might attract the police.

Bo Zhan, I feex heem. Crazy, evil old woman. Everyone hated her, even her own family. The women on the block said her daughter-in-law cried for a week when she learned she'd have to take Elizabetta in. Lizzie Caster, next door, had flatly refused to make room for her. No one cared what the old witch said.

On the other side of the bridge, the girls passed the old brick brewery, closed since the beginning of Prohibition years before, and crossed the street. They passed a block of small shops, a laundry, the card room where men loitered around the doorway for hours at a time, and finally the drugstore, which always smelled strongly of peppermint.

"Which magazine do we want?" Donna asked.

"You choose. You earned the dime," Quinn said. For a while, she forgot the old woman in black.

Four

After breakfast Tuesday morning, Uncle Dick and Justin loaded Uncle Dick's car with baskets of peaches. They would take them to the farmers' market near the waterfront in downtown Seattle. Quinn, with Amy, who was dressed for work, stood on the porch and watched them leave.

"Sometimes poor Uncle Dick's not much more help than Mr. Shadwell," Amy said. "If he's not careful, his bad back will go out on him again. I'll see if there's something in the drugstore downtown that might help him."

"The drugstore across the bridge ought to have those pills he was talking about the last time," Quinn said.

"I'd rather get the medicine downtown," Amy said quickly. "I'll pick it up during my lunch break so I won't be late getting home."

Quinn shrugged. It didn't matter to her, but Amy seemed determined to deal only with the pharmacist she knew.

After her sister left, Quinn crossed the street to work

on Miss Clotilde's cards again. The sky was overcast and the air smelled of dust and rain. Miss Clotilde had set up her materials on the kitchen table, in case rain really did fall.

"I need new specs," Miss Clotilde declared after an hour. She removed her wire-rimmed glasses and glared at them. "I tell you, Quinn, growing old carries two curses for every blessing."

Miss Ramona, unpacking groceries in the pantry, cackled a laugh. "Speaking of curses," she said. "I ran into old Mrs. DePiano on my way to the store. She was coming out of the church — I guess she'd been to early Mass. But it couldn't have done her any good. Heavens, but that woman is terrible! I thought she was going to hit me with one of her shopping bags — and I haven't the slightest idea why she was so angry with me. I can't understand half of what she says."

Quinn raised her head. "Donna and I saw her yesterday. She's always angry."

"Did you ever wonder what she carries in those shopping bags?" Miss Clotilde asked.

"I'm glad I don't know," Miss Ramona said, and she laughed.

"Grandma says she packs around all her belongings because she doesn't trust her son's wife," Quinn said. "But it must be hard, living with her son and his wife and nine kids."

Miss Clotilde shook her head. "I wish Father Mason

was still at the church. He would have done something about her. Or *for* her. I swear I think Father Sully eggs her on in her craziness. He keeps that whole parish in a hoo-hah most of the time over one thing or another, and he's been twice as bad since Roosevelt got elected."

"Father Mason was a saint," Miss Ramona said. "If he'd been here any longer, he might have made a Catholic out of me. He was good through and through." She folded up the paper grocery sack, put it away, and wiped her hands on her apron. "He was like Beau John, Quinn. Your dad has that quality of being genuinely interested in how everybody's getting along. And I love those stories of his. We surely do miss the walks he used to take around the neighborhood on summer evenings. The Pied Piper, we call him. Everybody wanted to follow him."

Quinn blinked back sudden, hot tears. "We miss him, too," she said.

"Well, he'll be back Saturday night, just the way he always is," Miss Clotilde said. "Why don't you run on home, dearie? We'll get at this job tomorrow, and I'm sure we can finish Thursday and get our money."

Quinn thanked her and left, and, to her surprise, found that Mr. Shadwell was sitting on the porch, rubbing his crippled hands together. He looked up at her, sighed, and shook his head.

"What is it, Mr. Shadwell?" she asked. "Is something wrong?"

He looked down at his old cracked shoes and shook his head again.

"Can I do something for you?" Quinn asked. Mr. Shadwell didn't speak, but he had many ways of making himself understood.

But not this time. He only shook his head again, and when he looked up at Quinn, it seemed to her that he was close to weeping.

She turned back and opened the screen door. "Miss Clotilde, I think something's wrong with Mr. Shadwell."

The old lady darted out the door and leaned over Mr. Shadwell. "What is it?" she asked him. "What's wrong?"

But Mr. Shadwell got to his feet and stumbled away into the orchard. He didn't look back.

Miss Clotilde sighed. "He gets moody sometimes. I'll bring his lunch out to him in his own little place and see to it he takes a good nap this afternoon."

Quinn left, remembering how sad Mr. Shadwell had looked when Beau John drove away Sunday evening. Her father would know how to help Mr. Shadwell. He knew how to help everyone.

Uncle Dick and Justin returned. From the kitchen window, Quinn saw Justin climbing a tree. Uncle Dick hosed dust off the car and whistled tunelessly.

"Will you do me a quick favor?" Auntie Sis asked as she sliced tomatoes on the cutting board.

"Sure."

"Will you run over to Mrs. Caster's? She borrowed your mama's sheet cake pan weeks ago, and if she's done with it, I'd like it back. I'm in the mood to bake, since it's not so hot today and I don't have to worry about heating up the kitchen. A nice big yellow cake with chocolate frosting sounds good, doesn't it?"

"That's Beau John's favorite," Quinn said. "But there won't be any left by Saturday night."

"Shucks, I'll make another one Friday night. How's that?"

"Perfect," Quinn said. But she couldn't smile.

That awful stranger! If only he hadn't come to talk to Beau John! Quinn couldn't keep him off her mind long enough to feel any peace at all.

What if everything she'd imagined was true? Beau John a smuggler? He could be caught by the police. What about Mama? She wasn't well enough for that kind of trouble. What about Feep, who adored his father?

Stop thinking! she ordered herself.

Quinn knocked on the front door a long time before Mrs. Caster finally answered. Her long nose was red and her eyes were bloodshot. Quinn asked for the pan, stammering a little.

Mrs. Caster stared at her. "Pan?"

Quinn nodded. "Auntie Sis hopes you're done with it."

Mrs. Caster blurted, "There was a time when your auntie would run over here to get the pan herself and stay for coffee with me. Nothing's the same anymore, not since Betty took up with that Mike and everybody talks about us behind our backs. If Mr. Caster were still alive, this would kill him."

"Nobody talks about you," Quinn babbled, wishing it were true. This was horrible! What was wrong with the woman?

"Your mother is so lucky, having Beau John for a good influence on her children. You and Amy would never take up with somebody like Mike. I swear I don't know what I'm going to do."

Quinn saw that Betty had come up behind her mother and had heard what she said. She was appalled and backed up a step. Betty moved forward, red-faced and eyes averted, and shut the door in Quinn's face.

Quinn was uncertain about what she was expected to do. Would Mrs. Caster bring the pan or not? She could hear Betty's voice inside, sharp and defiant. After several moments of indecision, Quinn went home empty-handed and told Auntie Sis what had happened. Mama and Grandma, who'd been cleaning closets upstairs, came down to add their comments.

"Mrs. Caster's going to pieces," Grandma said. "That wretched Betty with her bleached hair and her gangster boyfriend has driven her to it."

"Well, Lizzie Caster won't get any peace from talking to her dreadful old mother," Mama said. "But Mrs. Payne says Elizabetta and Lizzie are thick as thieves again and going to church together nearly every day and never missing those Save America for the Honest Americans meetings."

"I suppose Lizzie Caster will be making evil eye signs next," Auntie Sis said.

"It's catching, you say?" Grandma asked, and the women laughed.

Mama sat down at the table. "I hate to sound selfish, but I wish Lizzie had gone melancholy *after* she returned our pan. I can't afford a new one."

All of them laughed again, and Auntie Sis said, "Never mind. I'll make a round cake. It'll be just as good."

"Beau John will be sorry he missed it," Grandma said.

"I already promised Quinn I'd bake another for him next weekend," Auntie Sis said.

"And we'll serve it on the new plates we're going to win tomorrow night at the movies," Mama said. "I've got a hunch about this."

Amy came home with a bottle of thick white tablets for Uncle Dick's bad back and a small sack of hard candy for Quinn and Feep to share after dinner.

"You shouldn't spend your hard-earned money on candy for those kiddies," Grandma told her as she set the kitchen table for the meal.

"I didn't," Amy blurted, and then her face turned red.

Grandma and Quinn turned to stare. Feep, who had no interest in who paid for what, grabbed the sack out of his big sister's hand and peered inside.

"It was a gift," Amy added.

Mama, who had been busy in the pantry, stuck her head out the door. "A gift from whom?"

"Mama," Amy implored.

"We need to know whom we should thank," Mama said briskly.

Amy rolled her eyes. "Mama, may I speak to you privately?"

"I can see what's coming," Grandma said. Quinn couldn't tell if she was laughing or not, because she turned her head away.

"What's coming?" Quinn asked.

But Mama and Amy didn't answer. Instead, Mama followed Amy into the parlor and they shut the door. A few moments later, they returned, and Amy walked briskly toward the hall. Quinn heard her high heels clicking on the steps as she ran upstairs.

"Well?" Grandma asked.

"Never you mind," Mama said. She was smiling. "Amy will tell you when she's ready."

“Amy’s got a boyfriend, Amy’s got a boyfriend,” Feep shrieked.

Auntie Sis snatched at him, but he escaped out the back door, still chanting.

“Does she?” Quinn asked Mama, more shocked than pleased.

“Does she what?” Mama responded as she scrubbed potatoes at the sink.

“I give up,” Quinn said, exasperated. “I won’t ask any more questions.”

“Well, I’ll ask,” Auntie Sis said briskly. “Is he doing the right thing and coming for dinner some Sunday to meet Beau John?”

“Yes,” Mama said. “This Sunday, as a matter of fact. You’ll all find out his name at the same time.”

“And we’ll eat on your new plates,” Grandma said with satisfaction. “It’s about time this family had some real luck.”

There wasn’t much that happened in the neighborhood that caused more excitement than the Wednesday night movies. For the last six months, the theater manager had given away exciting door-prizes — bags of groceries, boxed sets of dishes, and once a vacuum cleaner, won by ancient Elizabetta DePiano, who refused to accept it because she thought vacuum cleaners were powered by the devil. The rest of the

DePianos wanted it, but the manager, disgusted by the old lady's outpouring of verbal abuse, drew another ticket, and the wonderful machine went to pretty Mrs. Kirk, whose baby girl had amazed everyone by learning to walk when she was seven months old.

On the way to the theater, Quinn and Donna trailed behind Mama and Auntie Sis. Feep and two of his friends ran in circles around them, exasperating everyone. Grandma walked with the Dallas sisters, and Justin strolled with Uncle Dick, discussing baseball. Amy hurried along with Donna's parents — she worked in the same building with Donna's father, and they were deep in a serious discussion about the latest elevator accident, where the full car had fallen two floors and sent a dozen people to the hospital. The sun hung over the horizon and the sky glowed like a stained-glass church window.

"This is almost a perfect evening," Donna said, even though she scowled slightly. She was wearing her new hand-me-down shoes, which pinched. Her cousin's feet were half a size smaller. "Maybe Justin will walk home with us instead of Uncle Dick."

"Don't count on it," Quinn said.

The theater showed only one movie on Wednesdays. Afterward, but before the exciting drawings began, the audience had to sit through a newsreel, two cartoons, and a half-hour comedy. That night the movie was a grim story about smugglers, and after the third gun fight, Quinn crawled over the feet of everyone between her and the aisle and escaped to the lobby. She intended spending a few minutes in the ladies' restroom, gathering courage to face the rest of the movie. But Betty Caster, snugly outfitted in her maroon and gold satin uniform, grabbed her arm and stopped her.

"Why is that old man staring at me?" she demanded.

Quinn, in her turn, stared. "What old man?"

"The one who lives behind the Dallas sisters. You know him. Why does he stare at me?"

"Mr. Shadwell's *here*?" Quinn asked, astonished. "I didn't know he was coming."

"Sometimes he does, and he sits in the back," Betty said. "And he drives me crazy staring at me."

She gestured toward the heavy red velvet curtains that separated the lobby from the theater. Quinn had just come through them, and she hadn't seen Mr. Shadwell. But, to oblige Betty, she stuck her head through the opening in the curtain, and sure enough, Mr. Shadwell sat in an aisle seat. When he saw Quinn looking at him, he hung his head as if he was embarrassed.

Quinn backed up and turned to face Betty. "He's not bothering anybody," she said.

"Well, he's bothering me," Betty said. "And not just here, either. He's always creeping around the neighborhood, watching and listening."

"Mr. Shadwell?" Quinn exclaimed. "What are you talking about?"

Betty patted her dry, bleached curls. "Almost every night when Mike takes me home, that old man is watching from the corner across the street. Mike won't put up with it much longer, I can promise you."

"Mr. Shadwell wouldn't hurt anybody," Quinn said.

"You know him," Betty said. "You're a friend of his, so tell him to quit watching us." She grabbed Quinn's arm again. "Mike doesn't like it, and I bet you know he can make lots of trouble for anybody who bothers me."

"No, I don't know anything of the kind," Quinn said, jerking her arm loose. She was exasperated and wanted nothing except to get away from Betty.

"Just ask Beau John," Betty said. "You just ask your old man whether or not Mike knows certain people, important people."

Quinn hurried back into the dark theater. Her heart thudded so hard she wondered if it was audible to others. She found her row and edged back to her seat.

"Are you all right?" Donna asked.

"Mr. Shadwell's here," Quinn whispered.

"Really?" Donna asked. "That's nice. But he could have walked with us."

Quinn wanted to tell Donna what Betty had said about the old man, but she kept silent. What else could she do? Donna might ask too many questions.

Beau John knew about Mike's important friends?

* * *

The movie ended, and finally, after a newsreel, cartoons that amused only Feep and his friends, and a comedy that they had seen before, the house lights went on and door-prize drawings began.

But Quinn forgot to keep her fingers crossed for her family. She forgot everything but Beau John. And Mr. Shadwell.

Donna's mother won a sack of groceries, and laughed until she cried. Sticking out of the top of the sack was a box of chocolate-covered cherries, her favorite candy.

The last number drawn was Uncle Dick's. He won a set of dishes that came in four colors, and after he picked up the box from the edge of the stage, he ceremoniously put it in Mama's lap.

"I heard about Sunday," he said. "We're ready for company now."

When they left the theater, Quinn saw that Mr. Shadwell was gone. The infamous Mike, handsome as any movie actor and dressed in an expensive pin-striped suit, leaned against a brick wall, smoking a tailor-made cigarette and waiting for Betty.

He wouldn't be afraid of Lizzie Caster or Elizabetta DePiano. His uncle was rich — and dangerous. In the strange and frightening world where he lived, he was becoming important. But Beau John — Beau John! — was someone who could be ordered around rudely by a stranger at the back door in the middle of the night.

Had Mike nodded slightly to her when he saw her looking at him? Was he acknowledging her as Beau John's daughter?

A smuggler's daughter?

Five

Shortly before sunrise, an ambulance clanged past the house. Quinn had been dreaming, but afterward she couldn't remember if she'd been having a nightmare or one of those frustrating dreams where she searched for something she couldn't find and couldn't even describe. She sat up in bed, gasping, clutching her blanket to her chest.

In the pale morning light, she saw Amy at the window, struggling with the shade, which stubbornly refused to roll up.

"What is it? What is it?" Quinn cried, frightened half out of her wits.

"There's an ambulance in front of the DePianos'. Heavens, what's wrong? Half the family is out on the porch, yelling."

Quinn, hauling the blanket with her, went to the window. "There's Mr. DePiano. Goodness, he's already in his uniform. What time is it?"

Amy snatched up the alarm clock that sat on the dresser she and Quinn shared. "It's a quarter to six," she said. "I think Mr. DePiano usually leaves for the post office at five. Something awful must have happened."

Mama and Auntie Sis came through the open bedroom door. "What's going on? Who's screaming?" Auntie Sis asked.

"Old Elizabetta and her grandkids and Mrs. Caster," Amy said. "There's an ambulance parked in front of the DePiano house and . . . They're bringing out somebody on a stretcher. It's one of the children!"

"Oh, lord," Mama cried. "Sissie, let's get dressed and go see if we can help."

"What the Sam Hill is going on?" Grandma demanded from the door. Feep, rubbing his eyes, whined wordlessly behind her.

"An ambulance is taking away one of the DePiano kids," Amy explained.

Feep shut up instantly and stopped rubbing his eyes. "I hope it's Pete," he said. "He stole my best aggie."

"Get back to bed before I give you such a swat your rear end will think the house fell on it," Grandma barked. Feep backed away from Grandma and retreated to his room.

Mama and Auntie Sis rushed toward the stairs. Through the window, Quinn saw Donna's mother running down the sidewalk, with her coat thrown on over her nightgown and her graying hair still done up in curling rags. Moments later, Mama and Auntie Sis caught up with her in the small crowd that had formed around the ambulance. A man in a white jacket waved them back, and the ambulance, bell clanging again, drove away.

Amy's alarm clock went off in her hand, startling her and adding to the confusion.

Uncle Dick wandered into the room, pulling his bathrobe on inside out. "Is somebody dead?" he wheezed.

"No, no," Amy assured him quickly, and Quinn explained what had been going on.

"Last night at the movies, their mama left early with one of the little boys," Uncle Dick said. "He was having a hard time breathing."

"I didn't notice that!" Grandma exclaimed. "Well, aren't we awful! That all goes to show how selfish people get when their noses are out of joint about something. I've been hating that crazy old Elizabetta so much that my heart shrank. I'll get dressed . . ."

"There goes Mama and Auntie Sis," Amy said from the window. "And everybody else. And Elizabetta . . . Quinn! She's throwing rocks at them. She's hitting them! We've got to do something."

Amy ran out of the room barefoot, and Quinn followed. They reached the front porch just as Auntie Sis staggered up the steps, holding one hand to her bloody head. Mama caught up with her and, breathing hard, pulled her through the door. Behind them, Donna's mother fled, limping, toward home.

Elizabetta, fully dressed in black, threw one rock after another at Mrs. Payne's retreating form. Mrs. Caster came up from behind and grabbed her arm. With her free hand, Elizabetta struck her daughter across the face. Quinn thought the old woman must have had a rock in her fist, because Mrs. Caster's nose spouted blood.

"This is a nightmare," Mama cried as she helped Auntie Sis through the door. "Somebody has to do something."

A rock crashed through the parlor window, and shards of glass flew across the floor.

"I curse Bo Zhan!" Elizabetta howled. "Bo Zhan, zat devil! I curse heem!"

"Why is she yelling about Beau John?" Mama asked angrily. "He isn't even here! She can't be blaming him for whatever's happened at their house."

Elizabetta's son grabbed both her arms and held them behind her back. He shouted something at her and forced her back down the street.

Uncle Dick, who had made it to the bottom of the stairs, started back up as soon as he had a look at his weeping wife. "I'll get dressed and drive you to the hospital, lovey," he called back to her.

"We need Beau John!" Feep cried. "Why isn't he here? We need Dad!"

Amy and Quinn threw their arms around each other and sobbed.

Grandma appeared in the front hall, holding Feep's baseball bat. "I'm not nice like Beau John," she announced. "If that crazy old woman comes back, I'll knock her block off."

Suddenly they all began laughing, even Auntie Sis.

"Well, wouldn't Beau John make a story out of this!" Auntie Sis said.

Amy said she would go with Uncle Dick when he took Auntie Sis to the hospital, to keep them company. "It's only a few blocks away from my office," she said. "I can leave for work from there after Auntie Sis has seen a doctor."

"We should go over again and see if Mrs. Caster needs serious help," Mama said.

"She yelled 'go away' when I knocked," Grandma said. "Maybe she needs to be alone. Maybe she needs to do some serious thinking about what kind of people she spends her time with."

When Uncle Dick drove away, Quinn waved good bye from the safety of the porch, and then went back inside to help Justin and Mr. Shadwell clean up the broken glass in the parlor.

They had come over near the end of what Grandma called the biggest hoo-hah the neighborhood had seen since Mr. Forbes Stafford had run off with his son's fourth grade teacher, and Mrs. Stafford, never a patient woman, had thrown her husband's clothes into the front yard, poured kerosene on them, and set fire to them. The fire spread to the house, and that was why there was a vacant lot directly across the street from the Wagners', the lot where the DePianos had gathered blackberries for homemade wine until Elizabetta moved in with them.

"I'm sure sorry about all this," Justin said as he emptied a dustpan full of glass chips into the bucket Quinn held. "I helped my dad put in a new window once, so I can probably fix this one, if your uncle can drive me back from the hardware store with the glass." He glanced toward Mr. Shadwell, who was slowly sweeping bits and pieces of glass into a small pile on the hardwood floor. "He can't help much," Justin said softly. "But he wouldn't stay home."

"The neighborhood's usually . . . nicer," Quinn said, embarrassed. The ruckus wasn't the fault of her family, but she couldn't help but wonder if Justin might be disgusted.

"My mother says every neighborhood has somebody in it who ought to be chained up in their basement," Justin said soberly.

Quinn burst out laughing. "Did she really say that?"

Justin nodded. "Yeah."

"Does she have somebody in mind?"

Justin grinned. "Oh, sure. The lady who lives behind us. Mom says if that lady ever dies, she's taking a wooden stake and a mallet to the funeral and make sure she's really dead."

Quinn laughed until she had to wipe tears from her eyes. "I think I'd like your mother a lot," she said.

"I think she'd like you, too," Justin said, and then he blushed and quickly bent over his work.

Quinn was hopelessly charmed.

Uncle Dick brought Auntie Sis back a few minutes after Justin and Mr. Shadwell left. Both of them seemed depressed, and Auntie Sis pushed Mama's hand away when she wanted a closer look at her stitches.

"Never mind about me, dearie," Auntie Sis said. "You'll want to hear something right away."

Uncle Dick sat down heavily, took a deep breath, and said, "While I was waiting for Sissie, Mr. DePiano came through the waiting room. He'd been in the other part of the building, where the closed wards are. His little boy is in an iron lung. He has infantile paralysis."

"Polio," Auntie Sis said. "They're calling it polio now."

"Is it Pete?" Feep asked, tears starting in his eyes.

Auntie Sis nodded.

"I'm sorry about what I said," Feep cried. "I didn't really want anything bad to happen to him."

"Your being mad at him didn't make him sick,"

Mama said quickly. "He has a bad disease. Nobody has magical powers that can make somebody else sick."

"That mean old lady put a curse on Beau John," Feep said. "Maybe *she's* got magic."

"She's got an empty head, that's all," Grandma said. "Dick, I hope you told Mr. DePiano how sorry we are."

"Oh, yes, yes," he said. "The poor man said he was sorry about what his mother had done, too. We shook hands."

"What a day," Grandma said. She sat down heavily. "Well, Sissie, you go upstairs and have a good lie-down. You, too, Nancy. You're not looking so good. And Dick, if you'll give me a minute, I'll fix you a nice strong cup of coffee. That always makes you feel better."

"I've got to go over and help Miss Clotilde," Quinn said after Auntie Sis and Mama went upstairs. "She'll wonder what happened to me."

"I want you to stay home today," Grandma said quickly. "I need all my chicks under the same roof. I just wish I could get Amy and Beau John home, too. I don't want to have to worry about anybody."

Every Thursday, a letter from Beau John came in the first mail delivery. No one thought about it that day, so when the mailman dropped the letter in the front door slot, it lay there unseen for a few minutes. Then Quinn, brushing up the last of the glass, noticed the letter and grabbed it with a shout.

Her mother's name was written neatly in pencil, but inside, the letter would be addressed to all of them. Quinn waited while Mama opened the envelope carefully with Great-grandmother's silver letter opener. Then, while she read the letter to herself first, Feep held the envelope under running water until the three-cent stamp loosened. His father always printed a message especially for him in tiny letters under the stamp.

"'Find penny on sill,'" Feep read aloud. "Sill? Does he mean windowsill? Which one?"

Grandma laughed. "He means for you to have a treasure hunt."

Feep took off running.

"What does the letter say?" Grandma asked Mama.

"He says he's been working long hours on the dock, but he'll be home on time Saturday," Mama said, smiling as she read. When she finished, she put the letter on the kitchen table for everyone to take turns reading. The family wouldn't answer the letter because Beau John seldom spent more than one night in the same place, and he often slept in his car to save money.

"I wish today were Saturday," Mama said. "I feel so — I don't know. Threatened, I guess. A child in the hospital. That's a terrible thing. But there's something else wrong, too. That crazy old woman. She's scaring me to death, and something's got to be done about her.

Mr. DePiano can't seem to take hold of the situation. And there's something else."

"What's that?" Quinn asked warily.

"We should find some way of helping the DePianos, in spite of Elizabetta. Staying away from them now is cruel."

"I'll ask around the neighborhood and see what the others say," Grandma said. "We'll do what's right."

The day seemed to stretch out forever. Everyone had been hoping for rain until the window was broken. Now they hoped the rain wouldn't fall, but a light drizzle began after lunch and grew heavier throughout the afternoon. Justin and Uncle Dick brought a new pane of glass home and installed it easily. Neighbors came for coffee and gossip, and left again.

Justin lingered after he finished work on the window. He couldn't pick fruit while it was raining, and his aunts said they didn't have anything else for him to do. Donna came over halfway through the afternoon with warm doughnuts fresh from her mother's kitchen. Grandma made hot Ovaltine for the young people and left them alone in the kitchen.

"How's your mother?" Quinn asked her friend. "I saw she was limping this morning."

"She turned her ankle," Donna said. "She's fine now, she says."

Quinn felt Donna's foot nudge hers under the table. When she looked up from her plate, she saw Donna's eyes shift toward Justin.

"Justin," Donna said suddenly. "Did you know there's going to be a dance at the community center in two weeks?"

Justin nodded while he swallowed the last of his doughnut. "Sure. My aunts are going, so I'll tag along, I guess. They've already dug their fancy clothes out of a trunk in the basement. The whole cottage smells like mothballs."

"They never dance," Donna said. "They get all dressed up in fancy dresses my mother says are older than God, but all they do is sit with the other old people and talk about the rest of us."

Justin laughed, as she meant him to.

"Is Mr. Shadwell going?" Quinn asked. She couldn't look at them, but pretended great interest in the calendar on the kitchen wall.

"He never goes anywhere," Donna said.

"That's right," Justin said. "I think he goes to bed as soon as it's dark every night."

"He went to the movies last night," Quinn said.

Donna nodded. "But that was the first time, I'll bet."

Quinn wondered what they would think if they had heard Betty's complaints about the man. But she didn't dare tell them, because Betty had mentioned Beau John in that conversation. What if one of them mentioned Mr. Shadwell to Betty, and she repeated her threat about having Mike's friends stop Mr. Shadwell from watching her? She had said that those same friends were known to Beau John.

Was the stranger who had come to the house to talk to Beau John one of those men?

Six

On Friday, Quinn worked with Miss Clotilde for most of the day, finishing the place cards. When the weather turned warm after lunch, they moved to the table outside, and Miss Ramona supplied them with coconut cookies and countless glasses of lemonade sour enough to pucker their mouths.

Occasionally Quinn caught glimpses of Justin moving through the tall grass at the far end of the orchard. By noon, he had stacked a dozen boxes of ripe peaches beside the gate, waiting for Uncle Dick to move them to the farmers' market in time for Saturday shoppers. A cloud of wasps, hungry and dangerous, glimmered above the boxes.

At last Miss Clotilde heaved a great sigh. "Done!" she announced, and she took off her glasses. "How about you, dearie?"

Quinn lettered the last name on the last card, blew on it to dry it, and added it to her pile. "I'm done, too," she said.

Miss Clotilde gathered the cards together, packed

them in an empty box, and pressed down the lid. "I'll hurry and change clothes. I should make it to the store before they close at five, and then, my dear, we'll be paid for our talents."

Quinn, rubbing her cramped hand, said, "I didn't think we'd finish in time."

"I had absolute faith in us," Miss Clotilde said.

Miss Ramona gathered up the glasses and empty plates. "I didn't want to disturb the two of you, but I heard that little Pete's parents were allowed to visit him for a minute or two, and he smiled at his mama. Some of us want to help them out in this awful time — bring food and flowers, and do what we can. I know the people in their church are helping, but the rest of us should, too. We've known the parents for a long time."

"The parents aren't the problem," Miss Clotilde said as she put her cherished pens back in their slender sandalwood box. "It's that vile old Elizabetta who's the problem. I can't imagine what she'd do with food we brought over. She'd think it was poisoned. But I'm willing to try if you are, sister."

"Then I'll make an extra casserole for them while I'm fixing our dinner," Miss Ramona said.

Quinn stood up and stretched to ease the ache between her shoulders. "If there's nothing else, Miss Clotilde, I'll go on home."

Miss Clotilde called out goodbye as she hurried into

the house. Miss Ramona walked to the gate with Quinn, talking more to herself than to anyone else about her intentions in the kitchen.

"All done?" Justin asked.

He and Mr. Shadwell sat together on the low grassy bank outside the fence. The boxes of peaches were gone — Uncle Dick had come for them half an hour before — and they deserved the rest they were taking.

"All done and going home," Quinn said. Immediately she felt like an idiot. Where else would she go but home?

Justin got to his feet. "Mr. Shadwell was wondering about your dad."

Quinn stopped in her tracks. It seemed to her for a moment that her heart had stopped. "What about Beau John?" she asked quickly.

Mr. Shadwell was struggling to his feet and taking forever to get there. When he finally stood erect, Quinn saw that his face was twisted with anguish.

Justin looked puzzled and uncomfortable. "He wondered when he was coming home again. He wanted me to ask you."

"Mr. Shadwell *talked*?" Quinn blurted, and then hated herself. Mr. Shadwell never talked. No one knew if he could.

Justin looked as embarrassed as Quinn felt. "No, no," he said. "But he makes himself understood by pointing. You know." He glanced over at the old man. "I'm sorry we're talking about you, Mr. Shadwell. We shouldn't be so rude."

Quinn was humiliated. She reached out to touch Mr. Shadwell's arm. "I'm sorry, too. You wondered about Beau John? We got a letter from him, and he said he'd be home Saturday night, just like always."

Mr. Shadwell nodded, but he didn't look relieved.

"I'll walk across the street with you," Justin said abruptly, and he took Quinn's arm, pulling her a little.

When they reached Quinn's gate, he murmured, "He's been upset all week, and got worse today. I thought it was about that little boy who was taken away in the ambulance, but he shook his head when I asked him."

"Why should he worry about my father?" Quinn asked.

What does Mr. Shadwell know about Beau John?

"Your dad's really nice to him," Justin said. "Sometimes he brings him black bread that the rest of us don't like."

"He does?" Quinn exclaimed. "I didn't know that. Beau John never said a word."

"He gets it at that bakery next to the card room on the other side of the bridge."

Quinn shook her head, mystified. "We don't buy anything there. Mostly they have European kinds of bread — coarse, you know. And so dark. Where is Mr. Shadwell from?"

Justin shrugged. "Beats me. My aunts think he doesn't like the bread so much as he likes the visit from your father."

Quinn could understand that. Everyone loved Beau John.

But what would they think if they knew his secret?

"Beau John will be here Saturday night," she said, hoping she was right. "I'll tell him Mr. Shadwell's been worried about him." She looked up at Justin, who seemed to have grown so much since last summer.

His face was so tan. His eyes glimmered like jewels.

Quinn blinked and looked away.

"Does your family still go to the movies on Saturday nights?" Justin asked suddenly.

"Not since Beau John began staying away all week," Quinn said. "Saturday is the only night he's home, and we like to sit together and talk."

"Do you have plans to go tonight?" Justin said.

Quinn gawked at him. What was he really asking?

She shook her head slowly. "No, I wasn't planning on going tonight. Donna and I . . ." She almost told him that they planned on choosing their school clothes that evening. He'd think they were as silly as grade school babies.

Could it be that he was about to ask her to go to the movie with him?

"I've already seen the movie that's playing there now," Justin said. "I saw it when it was playing downtown. It's not very good, so you aren't missing much."

He nodded to her, grinned, and loped back across the street, to follow Mr. Shadwell to the house.

Quinn pushed open the gate, still puzzled about what had actually just happened. But her greater concern was for Beau John. Could Mr. Shadwell have seen the man who had come to talk to Beau John last weekend? It was possible, since according to Betty, he prowled around the neighborhood in the middle of the night.

Quinn's mother was snapping green beans at the sink. "All done with the place cards, Quinn?"

"Yes, thank goodness. I was beginning to think half of Seattle is going to that dinner. Guess what, Mama? Miss Ramona said she's fixing the DePianos a casserole."

"Sis baked a mountain of cookies for them this afternoon — and in all this heat, too — but she didn't dare take them to the house." Quinn's mother added water to the pot of beans and set it on the stove. "She gave them to Mrs. Caster to deliver."

Quinn pulled a chair out from the table and took a deep breath. "Why does the old woman hate us?"

Mama shrugged and looked over at Quinn. "I don't have the faintest idea what brought on this last harangue. I know that she doesn't like people who aren't Catholic, but ever since her older son died, back there in Chicago, she's been more than a little crazy."

"But her son was killed a long time ago," Quinn argued.

"You don't get over losing a child. No, you don't get over it." Mama blinked away tears, and Quinn felt a catch in her throat, too. She barely remembered Feep's twin, but thinking of him always made her sad.

However, old Elizabetta's son had been a gangster, shot by another gangster in an argument in a Chicago alley. Did a mother grieve so much for a son that bad? She thought of asking Mama and decided she shouldn't. Maybe it didn't matter to a mother what her son had been like.

"Elizabetta's son getting shot didn't have anything to do with us," Quinn did manage to say, though. And to herself, she added, "And not with Beau John, either."

"No, of course not," Mama said. She brushed her forehead with the back of her hand. "I've wondered if she doesn't resent our whole family because Grandma's here with both her sons, and some of that resentment just spills over on your father. Of course, everybody knows why she hates Betty's Mike."

"Oh, well, him," Quinn said, dismissing Mike with contempt. "He's a gangster, the way her son was."

But she couldn't hide from what Betty had told her at the theater Wednesday night.

"Heavens above," Mama said, watching her curiously. "You look like a goose just walked over your grave."

Quinn jumped up, anxious to get out of the room and away from her mother. "Maybe one did," she said. "But I just remembered that I left my best blouse soaking in the laundry tub this morning."

"Auntie Sis rinsed it out for you," Mama said. "It looks as good as new. Is Donna bringing over that catalog after dinner?"

"Yes," Quinn called out as she started up the stairs to her room.

She passed Feep on the landing. "I heard that Pete's parents got to see him today," she said.

Feep cleared his throat as if he'd been crying. "I hope he gets better — but he still stole my aggie."

Quinn stopped and watched her brother continue down the steps. "Being mad at somebody doesn't make them sick, Feep," she said.

"What do you know?" Feep said, and he cleared his throat again.

Poor little kid, she thought. Pete's an awful brat — but he didn't deserve what happened to him. Think of being shut up in an iron lung, maybe forever! She'd seen iron lungs in the newsreels. What could be worse than knowing you couldn't breathe without one?

When Beau John gets here, Quinn thought, I'll tell him that Feep thinks it's his fault Pete got sick. He'll be able to talk to Feep the way nobody else can. She remembered the conversation her father and brother had when Feep had been so frightened by Elizabetta's sign of the evil eye. Beau John told a really good story about how nobody can do magic after they're old enough to know for sure that the sun will come up tomorrow.

Beau John would be home in just a little more than twenty-four hours. Everything would be all right then.

Donna brought the Sears and Roebuck catalog with her when she arrived at six-thirty. Quinn's family still sat at the kitchen table, scraping up the last of the orange sherbet Uncle Dick had brought home.

"I'd offer you some," Mama told Donna. "But we're such pigs that we ate it all."

Donna patted her stomach. "I'm full of homemade ice cream," she said. "Mama made some for the DePianos, but Elizabetta answered their door and wouldn't take it, so we got to eat it ourselves. My dad says there's some good to Elizabetta after all."

Everyone laughed, especially Auntie Sis. She touched her stitches gingerly and said, "I hope you're right. I've been wishing that this will take away my gray hair."

"Oh, I wouldn't bet on that, lovey," Mama said. "Even being beaned by Elizabetta won't call up a miracle. You're stuck with growing older, just as I am."

* * *

When the rest of the family gathered in the parlor to listen to the radio, Quinn and Donna sat at the kitchen table under the bright light and studied the women's section of the catalog, page by page. Each had been promised ten dollars for school clothes, less than they'd been given the year before because times were harder, but still enough to provide a new winter coat, a skirt, and perhaps two blouses. The three fifty-cent pieces that Miss Clotilde brought over for Quinn lay on the table, guaranteeing her new shoes.

"I'll be getting all my cousin's sweaters because she gained so much weight," Donna said as she turned a page carefully. "They're absolutely hideous. Her grandmother knitted them out of some awful old wool with chips of wood in it."

Quinn laughed. "That's wool straight from the sheep," she said. "The Dallas sisters have bed socks knitted out of horrible brown wool with bits of sticks and grass in it. And it's oily, even after it's been washed."

"I haven't worn bed socks since I was ten," Donna said. "Why would you think they'd want to?"

Quinn shrugged. "They're very strange ladies, but I like them. And I like their earrings, too."

"But not their old lace-trimmed corset covers," Donna said, laughing. "Mama says once they forgot one 'way back in the orchard and a bird built a nest in it. They didn't want to disturb the bird so they left it hanging out there until the end of summer."

"At least it wasn't bloomers," Quinn said.

The pages turned crisply, and from the other room, Quinn heard the sounds of radio voices and static, then music. "Mad About the Boy" was playing again.

Justin . . .

"Quinn, I've got something to tell you and I don't know how," Donna said suddenly.

Quinn raised her gaze from the page. Donna's tone was so serious that Quinn forgot to breathe.

"Look, it's like this," Donna said, blinking nervously. "Dad's pay was cut again. Mom has to quit her afternoon job at the dry cleaners because Grandma is coming to stay with us, and she's awfully sick." She averted her gaze and studied the glass-fronted cupboards as if she hadn't seen the contents hundreds of times before.

"Quinn, I'm not going to buy school clothes," she said. "I'm not going back to school." She spoke in a rush, her words falling over each other, as if she was afraid that if Quinn interrupted her, she wouldn't be able to finish. "There's a man in Dad's office whose brother works for *The Star*, and they need an errand girl, and this afternoon I went downtown and met the man in Dad's office, and he took me over to the newspaper and . . . Quinn, they gave me the job. I start

Monday morning. I won't need school clothes. Mama and I already picked out an office dress for me."

Quinn swallowed painfully. She had never dreamed that such a thing could happen. She and Donna had always planned to finish high school and then take a secretarial course. They would have more training than Amy. They would be among the privileged women Amy spoke of who took shorthand and sat at desks by windows instead of dark cubbyholes behind file rooms. They planned to live together in an apartment in the women's hotel downtown. One day they might even own a car. And when they finally married, they would pay for their weddings with their own money, and even buy their own furniture. Every year, after they chose their school clothes, they turned to the section of the catalog that featured household furnishings. Yes, they would have this sofa and that small table, this lamp and that set of glass dishes. Donna's bedroom furniture would be mahogany. Quinn's would be made of the modern bleached wood.

"You'll be an errand girl?" Quinn asked finally. "That's what you want?"

"It won't be forever," Donna said. She still couldn't look at Quinn. "The man — Mr. Hodges — he said that the paper has two women reporters and both of them started out as errand girls and one of them didn't finish high school."

"You'd like that," Quinn said quietly. "You like working on the school paper."

"I'll miss you," Donna said. Her round brown eyes filled with tears. "I'm sorry, Quinn."

A strange silence fell over them. For the first time in their lives, they had run out of things to say and share. Quinn was afraid that the happiest relationship she had ever known was drawing to a close.

Uncle Dick barged into the room and pulled open the refrigerator door. "Hey, girlies, did you drink up all that cold water? We're thirsty. Nope, here it is."

He took the frosted pitcher of water off the shelf and closed the refrigerator door with his elbow.

"I'll bring some glasses in for everybody," Quinn said. Her mouth was dry. She got to her feet and opened the cupboard door. Once they'd had matching glasses, but as they broke, one by one over the years, they had been replaced by odd, unmatched glasses Mama found at end-of-the-month sales at the dime stores downtown.

She put the glasses on an old painted tray and followed Uncle Dick through the swinging door to the parlor. Her family — except for Beau John — sat around the table and a half-finished game of dominoes. The radio murmured and murmured. Uncle Dick filled the glasses from the pitcher, and Quinn passed them out.

When she returned to the kitchen, Donna was gone. She had left the catalog behind.

Quinn sat down and stared at the drawings of blouses on the page before her.

When Beau John got home, she'd ask him to take a walk with her, and then she'd tell him what had just happened. He would know what to do and say.

He would know what she should think about this terrible loss.

Seven

There had been a time when Quinn would have told her family immediately about Donna's surprising plans. The family, sitting around the parlor table, would have discussed it, argued about it, and eventually accepted the change and the effect it would have on Quinn. But that evening she went upstairs without saying a word to anyone except, "I'm awfully tired, so I'm going to bed."

No one should have two bad things to deal with at the same time, she thought, especially if those things involved the two most important people in her life. She needed Beau John to help her deal with the feeling that Donna had abandoned her and joined the ranks of grown women without warning, leaving her behind in girlhood.

And she needed Donna just as much, to help her with her fears for Beau John.

But she hadn't told Donna what she had overheard her father saying to the stranger! She hadn't told anyone.

She spent several minutes at her bedroom window, watching the sky turn dark, listening to the fading chatter of birds. There were more roosting in the neighborhood trees now than there had been a week before. In another two weeks, flocks would begin forming for the long flight south.

The first signs of fall were close. The vine maples on the hill behind them would turn red and gold first, and then the birch trees would splash the woods with yellow jeweled leaves.

Quinn's school clothes would arrive, hard new shoes that wouldn't feel right at first, and a stiff wool coat that smelled of strong dye and leather buttons.

But Donna would be working for the newspaper, spending her days in unimaginable, glamorous labor to bring out the pages Quinn's family pored over after dinner.

She went to bed and fell into a restless sleep. Later, she woke and caught the scent of cake baking. Auntie Sis was making a cake for Beau John.

Amy splashed water in the bathroom next door to their bedroom, humming softly. She was seventeen, and one could expect her to take on the role of a grown woman. But Donna was only fifteen! It wasn't fair! It wasn't fair!

Quinn swung her legs out of bed and padded across the bare floor to the window. The shade stuck stubbornly for a moment, and then clattered and flapped wildly, but it rolled to the top. Quinn pushed the window open as far as it would go and leaned out.

She saw Mr. Shadwell immediately. He stood diagonally across the street, out of reach of the glow cast by the streetlight, but clearly visible to Quinn because he was silhouetted in front of the Casters' parlor windows. If he had moved only a few feet north, he would have become invisible before the vacant lot.

What was he watching? He was facing down the street, where the DePianos lived. When Amy turned off the water in the bathroom, Quinn could hear the hysterical rise and fall of Elizabetta's voice and the deep growl of her son's.

I hate her for cursing Beau John! Quinn thought. How dare she! Look how her curse backfired. Her own grandson lies in an iron lung, and he might die. Surely his young life was ruined.

Beau John told a story that he swore was true. When his father was young, he had known a shoemaker who made the most beautiful shoes in the whole county, wonderful shoes crafted out of leather in every color imaginable. But no one ever bought them and the shoemaker couldn't understand why. He was a cranky man at the best of times, and his failing business made him even more difficult. In the evening after he closed his shop, he would climb the steps to his little apartment, open a window, and throw cold water and trash on the people who walked along the street below. When he fell on a patch of ice and hurt himself, everyone said, "He got what he deserved."

A new shoemaker came to town and set up shop down the road. He wasn't very talented, but he did his best, and he worked hard to please his customers. At night when his shop was closed, he sat on a rickety wooden chair in his doorway and greeted the people who passed by. When he caught pneumonia, his neighbors brought him food and ran his errands, and everyone said, "How terrible that such a good man should be so ill. It isn't fair."

No one would care if Elizabetta got sick. Everyone would care about Beau John.

Unless they learned his secret.

Suddenly her attention was drawn back to Mr. Shadwell. He moved more quickly than she thought he could, and in a moment he had disappeared into the brush growing in the vacant lot.

Had he seen her watching? Probably. She felt embarrassed at catching him watching the neighbors, since she was doing the same.

Amy came into the bedroom, fingering the curling rags in her hair. "What's going on outside?" she asked when she saw Quinn out of bed.

"I heard Elizabetta yelling about something," Quinn said as she pulled down the shade and returned to bed.

"When isn't she?" Amy said. She sat on the edge of her bed and leaned forward to snap her small lamp on.

In the soft light, her face looked almost as young as Feep's.

"Quinn, I need your advice," Amy said.

Quinn sat up. "What's wrong?"

Amy sighed. "You know that someone is coming to dinner on Sunday to meet the family."

Quinn nodded. "Your mysterious boyfriend. I still haven't figured out when you had time to meet him — and when you spend any time with him."

Amy unwrapped an unsatisfactory curling rag before she answered. "We have lunch together nearly every day," she said. "Sometimes on Saturdays — well, Quinn, I get off at two on Saturdays, you know — sometimes we go for walks. Or to a movie matinee, but we only stay for one feature."

"Amy!" Quinn's voice raised with shock. "Mama doesn't know *that*, does she?"

Amy shook her head and began rewinding the curl. "No, no, of course not. She had enough to take in when I told her . . ."

"Told her what?"

Amy let her hands fall in her lap. "Carl — Carl Mercer's his name — Carl is lots older than I am."

"How much older?" Quinn asked, shocked again.

"Ten years. And don't make that face, Quinn! Beau John is nearly ten years older than Mama."

It was true. But that was different. Quinn didn't know why, but it just was, and she said so.

"Quinn, Mama was only eighteen when she married Beau John. I'll be eighteen next February."

"You're getting married!" Quinn cried.

"No, no, no," Amy babbled. "Not yet, anyway. Stop shouting, or Mama will come upstairs and want to know what's going on."

"You have to tell her everything," Quinn said. "You can't be planning on getting married . . ."

"He hasn't asked me!" Amy said. She covered her face with her hands. "I think he might, after he meets everybody. I think he might ask me pretty soon."

"Good grief," Quinn said. She pulled her pillow to her chest and hugged it. "This is crazy. Where did you meet somebody that old? In your office? Is it somebody from your office? I'll bet you didn't tell Mama that, because she would be horrified, Amy! You can't be having a romance right in front of the people you work with! Mama and Auntie Sis warned you about that!"

"No, he isn't from the office." Amy bit her lip. "He's the pharmacist in the drugstore downstairs in the building, and Mama knows all about it."

Quinn was speechless. The only pharmacists she had ever seen were ancient men who looked as if they had scrubbed themselves so hard and so often that their skin seemed nearly transparent. And they smelled of chemicals, like doctors.

"This is what I wanted to ask you," Amy said. "I

know the rest of the family is expecting somebody my age, so nobody is taking this seriously."

"Of course they're taking it seriously," Quinn said. "I heard Mama and Auntie Sis talking about what they're going to cook."

"I'm not talking about food," Amy said. "I'm talking about how everybody dresses."

"What do you mean, how everybody dresses?" Quinn said. "We always dress up when we have company for dinner."

"Not really," Amy said. She groaned. "Uncle Dick thinks he's dressed up if he puts on a tie."

"Well, he is!" Quinn argued.

"I want him and Beau John to wear jackets to the table."

Quinn stared. "But it's so hot! Beau John might do it but Uncle Dick won't."

"He has to," Amy said emphatically. "Uncle Dick and Beau John and Feep have to wear their suits."

"When they find out that you want them to wear suits to dinner in their own house in August so they can meet an old man . . ."

"He's not old!" Amy cried. "He's twenty-seven."

"That's old!" Quinn said. "That's more than old enough to shave! Ugh! It makes my skin crawl to think about it."

Amy stared at her. "What on earth are you talking about?"

Quinn shuddered and hugged her pillow closer. "It makes me sick to think about you sneaking into a movie with an old man who has to shave . . ."

"Men shave!" Amy shouted. "All men have to shave! Quinn, I think you're going crazy. What a dumb thing to say!"

Mama opened the door, startling both of them. "What in heaven's name are the two of you shouting about? What's this about men shaving? Am I going to like hearing about this conversation, girlies?"

Both girls averted their gaze and found much to interest them across the room.

"Girls?" Mama persisted.

"Sorry, Mama," Amy said. "Sorry."

"Sorry," Quinn echoed.

"Well, I should hope you would be," Mama said briskly. Her fair face was red and her breathing was labored. When she was upset, her heart beat too hard and she had trouble catching her breath. Her daughters knew that she had nearly died from rheumatic fever after Feep's twin brother died. They tried not to aggravate her.

Mama went out and closed the door quietly behind her. Quinn and Amy stared at each other.

"You're such a baby," Amy said seriously. "I worry about you. I know you have a crush on Justin — and he's a darling boy. But he's only a baby, too. You'll see. You'll lose interest in him when you meet somebody . . ."

"Stop," Quinn said. "Don't say anything more. I don't want to think about things like that."

Amy opened her mouth as if she was going to continue her lecture. But then she laughed. "Oh, Quinn. I'm sorry I brought any of this up. I know you still play with our dolls up in the attic, and I think that's so sweet and dear. You stay just the way you are, and don't waste time thinking about the rest of the world. Please? If at the worst times in my life I can always picture you all nice and safe, setting the doll table with the little rosebud cups Grandma gave us that Christmas after Feep was born, then the world won't seem like such a bad place."

A week before, Quinn would have said, "It's not a bad place." But she didn't believe that any longer.

Quinn sighed deeply. "If you want Uncle Dick to dress up on Sunday, you'd better give him plenty of notice. Tell him before you leave for work in the morning, so he'll have all day to mull it over."

"And can I count on you to get Feep into his suit?"

"I'd rather die, but I'll do it."

"Fine. Wonderful." Amy smiled, turned out her light, and snuggled into her bed. "And you'll wear your white dress with the lace collar, won't you?"

Quinn gritted her teeth. "No, I'm going over to the

Dallas sisters and borrow some of their finery. Maybe I'll see if Miss Ramona will let me wear that old maroon velvet dress of hers, the one with the dust ruffle and the black bead fringe. Of course, I'll need a corset so I can get into it. And Miss Clotilde's black lace gloves with the holes in the fingers that she mended with white thread."

"Oh, Quinn, you're the best sister anybody ever had," Amy said, laughing.

The thought of Amy's marrying someone and going away was more than Quinn could bear.

By the time Quinn went downstairs the next morning, Amy had left for her office and breakfast was nearly over. Only Grandma and Feep were still in the kitchen.

"What plans do you have for today?" Grandma asked her.

Quinn shrugged. "No plans, Grandma. Do you need anything done?"

"Nope," Grandma said. She refilled Feep's milk glass and put the bottle back in the refrigerator. "But you'd better ask your mother what she needs done, because she's planning on scraping every inch of the house today to get ready for tomorrow."

"Where is Mama?" Quinn asked.

"She and Sis dragged the parlor rugs out back for a good beating, and your mama knows she shouldn't be doing heavy work like that, but she won't listen to a word anybody else says. Dick will mow the lawn as soon as they're through. Big doings, and all for this stranger." Grandma shook her head. "I say he should take us just like we are."

"Me, too," Feep said. "I bet Dad won't wear a suit. I bet Dad won't even wear shoes!"

Quinn could tell by the furious expression on Feep's face that he knew arguing was hopeless and now he could look forward to nothing except being as disagreeable as he could manage.

Only Beau John could make Sunday dinner turn out right.

Quinn shivered suddenly, remembering her premonition that Beau John wouldn't come home.

She was being foolish. He'd come home. He always did.

But he didn't come. Saturday afternoon stretched out, hot and dusty, and the family waited dinner for Beau John because he usually made it home in time.

"Last week he missed dinner," Feep announced firmly while they were eating their slices of yellow cake. "Don't you remember? It's okay if he's not here yet."

But Quinn saw Mama's tense expression, the fine lines around her eyes that seemed deeper that evening, the blue tinge to her lips. "Mama, are you all right?" she asked. "You shouldn't have cleaned the rugs. I could have done it."

"You cleaned the rugs?" Amy asked Mama.

"They needed it," Mama said. "And I need a cup of tea. That always gives me a little boost."

Amy looked close to tears. Quinn touched her shoulder but didn't speak. Amy laid her hand over Quinn's and sighed.

Where was Beau John?

Auntie Sis dragged Feep off to bed at ten-thirty. Amy went upstairs afterward, claiming a headache. Grandma shuffled out to the porch and batted mosquitoes away with a sheet of newspaper folded into a fan. Quinn joined her, sitting on the top step in the dark. After a while, Uncle Dick came out to say good night. A few minutes later, Mama did the same.

"When Beau John gets here, tell him there's cold chicken for him in the refrigerator," Mama said. "I'm just too tired to stay up any longer."

She went inside and the screen door closed behind her.

"I don't believe my boy's coming," Grandma said suddenly in the dark.

Quinn gasped, but she said, "He'll come, Grandma."

"No," the old woman said. "I've got a funny feeling about it, Quinn. And I think you do, too."

Should she tell Grandma about the conversation she'd overheard the week before? No. Grandma was too old to find out that Beau John was a smuggler or a rumrunner. And she'd tell somebody, Uncle Dick at least. He was Beau John's brother and the man of the family when Beau John was away.

Grandma and Quinn sat in silence and listened to night noises. At midnight, they went inside, but Quinn came back downstairs half an hour later and sat on the porch alone.

Across the street, motionless in the dark, Mr. Shadwell waited with her. Hours later, when the eastern sky turned pale as the inside of a seashell and the first birdsong began, they nodded to each other and gave up.

Beau John had not come home. Quinn was sick with fear.

Eight

At breakfast, Uncle Dick offered a hopeful observation. "Maybe Beau John found some extra work," he said. "I know that every once in a while dock workers get chances to pick up a few more dollars."

"If we had a telephone, Beau John could call us," Amy said. "Lots of people could call us."

"Your boyfriend could call you," Feep said. "Justin could call Quinn."

"*You* could call nasty little Evangeline Potter who followed you home on your birthday and cried because you wouldn't let her in the house," Quinn said loudly.

"I *hate* Evangeline Potter!" Feep shouted. "Everybody hates . . ."

Quinn kissed the back of her hand noisily. "'Oh, Evangeline, I love you so much!'"

"Mama!" Feep screamed.

"Heavens, somebody stuff a pancake in that boy's mouth and shut him up before the neighbors call the police," Auntie Sis said sourly. "And you, Quinn, stop your teasing. Your mama's worn out."

Quinn flushed guiltily. Mama didn't look well that morning, and no one should do anything that would upset her.

"Sorry, Feep," she said quickly.

"Sorry, Quinn," Feep responded obediently. But he kicked her under the table to cancel the apology.

Quinn didn't flinch. Mama deserved extra consideration that morning.

By three o'clock, the house shone and the pork roast in the oven was nearly done. Feep and Uncle Dick, in their pressed suits, sat side by side on the parlor sofa, listening to the radio. The women made countless trips back and forth between parlor table and kitchen. They had used the best linen tablecloth and napkins, stiff with starch. They took silver flatware from the buffet, where it was stored between holidays. The new china was unpacked, washed, and given a special buffing with soft old flannel.

Donna, upon hearing the news about Amy, brought an armload of yellow roses. She and Quinn spoke only briefly, with much embarrassment, almost as if they were strangers, and Donna didn't stay long.

The Dallas sisters, who hadn't been told directly, nevertheless heard about the dinner from someone and contributed a silver candelabra, tall yellow candles, and an ornate silver vase for the roses.

"Now all we need is Beau John," Auntie Sis said as she stood, hands on hips, surveying the beautiful table.

"I think we'd better not set a place for him," Mama said. "It makes us look — I don't know — unorganized somehow. As if we don't know where our family members are. We can set a place fast enough if he shows up during dinner. I don't want Amy's friend to think people come and go in this house without anybody knowing anything ahead of time."

"But that describes us exactly," Auntie Sis said. "Because we never know about Beau John, and that's our fault, Dick's and mine. If we weren't here freeloading on you, Nancy, Beau John wouldn't have had to take that awful job to help support us . . ."

"Beau John had to take the job because he was out of work," Mama said firmly. "Even if you weren't here, Beau John would still be somewhere else today. And Sissie, don't you dare take away my pleasure in having you here with us. I can't imagine getting along without you."

"But . . ." Auntie Sis began. Her eyes filled with tears.

"Oh, sakes alive," Mama cried. "Let's not wish anything could be different from what it is. You know how Beau John feels about always doing your best right where you are, with whatever you find there. We're going to have a fine time this afternoon, and Amy's friend will think we are wonderful."

"My jacket itches and I'm going to take it off," Feep announced loudly from the sofa.

"If you mention that jacket one more time, I'll give you an itch you can't scratch," Grandma snapped. "And that goes for you, too, Dick."

Uncle Dick raised his hands in surrender. "Mother, I'll wear this horseblanket until the day I die," he said solemnly.

"Don't promise what you don't plan to deliver," Grandma said. "Mercy, look at that car out front! Is that your friend's car, Amy? Save us, but he's a rich man!"

Quinn watched the man walking briskly up to their porch. He was small and slight, with thin light brown hair and pale skin, and he wore a dark blue suit. He smiled when he saw her in the doorway. Even his eyes smiled.

"You're Quinn," he said pleasantly. "Amy told me wonderful things about you." He handed her the sack he carried. "Double-chocolate cookies," he said. "Amy said it's your favorite dessert. It's my favorite, too."

Oh, Beau John, she thought. I wish you were here — because he's *nice*!

She turned and saw Amy standing behind her, her expression uncertain.

"Here's Carl," Quinn said, smiling at her sister. "Right on time."

There were a few minutes of confusion while Amy tried to introduce her friend, everyone interrupted everyone else, and Mama, for no reason anyone could understand, began crying.

"Here, Mama, sit down on the sofa," Quinn babbled. Her mother's face was white, her lips blue.

"No, no, it's time for dinner," Mama protested, wiping tears away with the backs of her hands.

Carl Mercer moved swiftly to her side. "Please sit down for a while," he murmured smoothly. "Let those big girls of yours take care of the table. Sit with me."

Mama, who had always been stubborn, sat down obediently. Quinn saw Carl's hand slip from Mama's trembling fingers to her wrist.

"I don't know what's gotten into me," Mama gasped. "I'm just so happy to meet you, and so sorry Amy's father . . ."

"I know," Carl said. "But everything is wonderful." His eyes seemed unfocussed. Quinn knew he was counting Mama's pulse.

Amy stood in front of them, wringing her hands. "Carl, is Mama all right? Is she all right?"

"I believe we should call her physician," Carl said. He held Mama's hand between his own and looked earnestly into her face. "You won't mind, will you? Just a little chat on the telephone . . ."

"Carl, don't you remember that we don't have a phone?" Amy asked.

"I'd forgotten," Carl said and he shook his head. "Well, I'll drive someone to a telephone, then, and that person can speak for you, Mrs. Wagner. Who in your family knows the most about your health? When was the last time you saw your doctor?"

"Years ago!" Grandma cried. "She won't go. We try and try to get her to go, but she won't spend the money."

Mama leaned back. "But I'm fine. I only need to catch my breath."

Quinn saw a resigned expression flicker quickly on Carl's face and then disappear.

"Please don't make a fuss over me," Mama went on. "Girls, bring dinner to the table. Everybody, please sit down."

Carl leaned close to her. "Perhaps you . . ." he began.

Mama struggled to her feet. "I'm feeling much better now," she said. "Everyone, please. You're embarrassing me."

Carl looked to Amy for help, but Amy only shrugged and bit her lip. Who could do anything with Mama when she dug in her heels?

Auntie Sis and Grandma whisked the food to the table while everyone sat down. Mama was still too pale and her hands still trembled, but her smile didn't seem forced.

Quinn and Amy exchanged a nervous glance. Mama couldn't get sick now! Beau John wasn't home. What if something happened to her?

What if something had happened to Beau John? Quinn hadn't forgotten the most frightening parts of the conversation she had overheard. Beau John might have been hijacked. He might have been caught by the police.

"Quinn, please pass the butter."

Quinn's head jerked up and she stared at Grandma.

"Butter," Grandma reminded her.

Everyone laughed kindly, but Quinn was humiliated.

Dinner finally ended. It hadn't been a complete success, because everyone's concern for Mama left them uneasy. But the afternoon hadn't been quite as bad as Quinn had feared, either. Mama didn't eat much, but she talked a little and her smile seemed natural enough. Uncle Dick and Carl found they shared a common interest in airplanes, and Carl had actually flown in one for a few minutes one day. Feep peppered him with questions.

Auntie Sis and Grandma scurried back and forth to the kitchen, refilling platters, bowls, and water glasses. Quinn saw them watching Mama.

A thunderstorm broke over the neighborhood while Grandma served the cookies, and Uncle Dick got up to disconnect the antenna wire from the radio so that lightning couldn't follow it into the house.

"Mr. Mercer," Feep said loudly. "Mr. Mercer?"

"Yes, Feep?" Carl said.

"My friend Ed had a big white cat with green eyes, and lightning came down their antenna wire and the cat — his name was Scooter — the cat was sleeping next to the radio and the lightning knocked him off the table and he died right there in front of Ed's grandma who got apoplexy and she died, too, and they both got buried in the same hole. On a Saturday. The hole got rain in it."

There was a long silence.

"Thank you for that, Feep," Auntie Sis said calmly. "But you'll never be the storyteller your father is."

Everyone, even Feep, began laughing then, and the awkwardness that had plagued the dinner dissolved. When Carl left late that afternoon, he said, "I've never had a better time."

Quinn and Amy exchanged triumphant smiles.

Late that night, while the girls were undressing in their bedroom, Amy asked, "What did you really think of him?"

"He's nice," Quinn said. "He looks younger than you said he was."

Amy laughed a little. "But he shaves."

Quinn shook her head. "Don't tease me, Amy."

"I'm sorry. Sometimes you surprise me."

Quinn stared at her. "Sometimes you surprise me!"

Amy took her curling rags out of her top drawer and began the long process of rolling up her hair. "What do you suppose Beau John will think of Carl?"

"Oh, he'll like him," Quinn said. Her mood immediately turned bleak at the mention of Beau John's name. "He likes everybody."

"Quinn!" Amy cried. "Won't he like Carl better than other people?"

"Yes, yes," Quinn said. "Of course he will. He'll love Carl when he meets him."

Amy's gaze locked on Quinn's face. "Where do you suppose Beau John is?"

Quinn looked away, before Amy could see the fear in her eyes. "Uncle Dick thinks he got a chance for extra work."

Amy nodded slowly, sighing. "I suppose so. It seems so awful to me to have him gone all week. It's not good for Mama. I wish I made more money."

"You do the best you can," Quinn said. "Everybody tries."

Amy jumped into bed and snapped out her bedside light. Quinn raised the shade and pushed the window open as far as it would go. The blackberries in the vacant lot were ripe, and they scented the neighborhood. This was an hour to spend on the porch, under the scarf of the Milky Way, listening to Beau John weave stories.

Was her father somewhere out there under the stars, trying to get home?

Mike O'Hara's car rolled down the street, engine turned off, tires crunching gravel. It stopped in front of

Betty Caster's house. Betty got out alone and hurried to her porch. The car began rolling again, and halfway down the hill, the engine started. Betty slammed her front door.

A figure stepped out of the shadows. Mr. Shadwell again. He looked up at Quinn and raised his arm slowly. She waved back.

"Who's out there?" Amy asked.

Quinn flinched. She had forgotten Amy.

"It's only Mr. Shadwell," she said. She pulled the shade and got into bed.

"I wonder what he's doing out this late?" Amy said.

"It's a nice night," Quinn said. "Rain makes everything smell good."

"He's the strangest person."

"He must be all right because Beau John likes him," Quinn said.

"Oh, Beau John likes everybody," Amy said.

"So he'll like Carl," Quinn said. She grinned in the dark.

Amy threw a pillow at her and burst out laughing.

Nine

Mama didn't get up Monday morning. Auntie Sis and Grandma made breakfast, and they explained to the family that Mama was tuckered out from all the festivities on Sunday. This had happened before, but not often. Quinn ate her cereal in silence, grateful that she'd kept to herself what she suspected about Beau John's dangerous business.

The milkman brought their milk order and left again, complaining that the morning was already too warm for comfort. The bread man brought his tray to the back door, and in spite of Feep's noisy begging, Grandma only bought four loaves of bread and two dozen rolls.

Uncle Dick, frowning and nervous, left for the long drive to Tacoma. He had heard rumors over the weekend that the smelter might be hiring. Amy rushed out in a flurry of concern about missing her streetcar, because she had misplaced her gloves and taken forever to find them. Auntie Sis had a ten o'clock appointment with the owner of a small bakery in West Seattle. The baker was the cousin of a friend of the Dallas sisters, and he needed an extra cashier on Saturdays.

"I predict that we'll all be working before you know it and our hard times will be over," Auntie Sis said.

"I'm going to quit school like Amy did, but I'll get a job at the airport," Feep said. He wore a milk moustache.

"Of course you will," Grandma said. "Just as soon as you graduate from high school."

"Donna's family let her quit school and she's not as old as Amy," Feep said.

"Donna is still a big girl," Grandma said. "And her family is having a hard time, what with needing a new roof before winter."

"Quinn could lie about her age and quit school if she wanted," Feep whined. "You know she could. It's only me who has to stay in school for a million years."

"Quinn isn't quitting school," Grandma cried, exasperated. "Finish your breakfast, Feep, and then go clean up your room. Sometimes I think I hear something moving around in there when you aren't home. It makes scratching noises and . . ."

"Auntie Sis!" Feep bellowed. "Make her stop."

Auntie Sis, carrying bowls and spoons from the table to the sink, scowled at him. "There's probably a raccoon in your closet," she said. "Remember when your pa told us about his school friend who didn't open his closet door for a year and didn't know that a mama raccoon had chewed through the roof and was raising her family in there?"

Feep turned pale. "I don't want to look! Somebody else has to look!"

"Lord have mercy," Grandma muttered. "Feep, I'll give you five seconds to quit that racket and get upstairs. And don't you dare wake up your mama!"

"After I clean my room, can I go over to Monkey Jackson's? We're going to make get-well cards for Pete and give them to his dad to take to the hospital."

"Just make sure Elizabetta doesn't catch you hanging around their house," Grandma warned. "She was awfully quiet yesterday, and that's unusual for her. She could be brooding something, like a crazy old hen."

"Monkey says old Miz DePiano hates Beau John because he helped fix the porch for free over at the Baptist church," Feep announced from the doorway.

"What rubbish," Grandma said. She ran hot water into the dishpan and shook the soap holder in it. "She hates him because he isn't Catholic, just like she hates everybody else on this part of the hill. And before you quote Monkey's family to me anymore, I'd like you to remember that *his* mama hates everybody on the down side of the hill because they *are* Catholic. I'm surprised Monkey has a kind bone in his body."

"He doesn't have bones," Feep said. "He's all fat instead." With that, he disappeared noisily up the stairs.

"Lands' sakes," Grandma muttered over the dishpan. "Sometimes I think this neighborhood is the nicest place in the whole world, and then I get to thinking about all the undercurrents, and who won't speak to whom, and who hates this person or that person because of their church or their politics or the country where they came from, and I wonder what gives Beau John the crazy idea that the universe is harmless."

Quinn, listening at the table, blinked tears out of her eyes. "He wouldn't be Beau John if he didn't think things like that."

Grandma sloshed water vigorously. "How did I get such a dreamer for a child? He's no more like Dick than a songbird is."

Auntie Sis, wiping down the table, laughed. "Every family has a Beau John, thank goodness. Without them, we'd all end up killing each other. But goodness, I do wish we knew where he is. I'm getting to be like you, Grandma. It makes me nervous when I don't know exactly where everybody is."

"Well, there was another time when Beau John didn't get home when we thought he should," Grandma said. Her voice was falsely bright. "Remember?"

"That was back in June, and he got home early the next morning, Grandma," Quinn said. "He had car trouble."

Grandma sighed. "I know, I know. I'm only trying to

make myself feel better. My word, but I'm a spoiled woman. Just think about the mothers and wives of the poor men in Hooverville. Those men probably don't even have the price of a stamp so they can write home, and their families don't know if they're alive or dead. Now I've got the laundry all to myself today, and if I keep standing around here on one leg, whining, I'll be later hanging it out than the Dallas girls."

"I'll help, Grandma," Quinn said.

"Your mama doesn't want you anywhere near a wringer," Grandma said as she put the dishpan away.

"I can fetch and carry," Quinn said. She didn't want to be close to the wringer, either. Every woman on the hill knew someone whose hand was deformed because it had slipped into the wringer accidentally. Grandma and Mama used a long stick to feed wet clothes into the whirling, grinding rollers, but that stick had a frazzled end, showing proof of the times it, too, had slipped.

Grandma glanced over at her. "You feeling all right? You look pinched."

Quinn laughed. "What does 'pinched' mean?"

"I never did know," Grandma said. "It's what my own mother said to me."

Quinn got up from the table. "Well, I'm not 'pinched' or 'peaked' or even 'off my feed,' so I'll get dressed and bring down everybody's laundry."

"Mercy, here's Justin," Auntie Sis said. She opened

the back door as Quinn fled to hide on the stairs because she was still in her robe.

She heard him ask for her, but Auntie Sis told him he'd have to leave a message.

"Miss Clotilde wants to know if Quinn will work for her Wednesday if she goes downtown and gets another job for them," Justin said.

"I'll see she gets the message," Auntie Sis said. "My, my, Justin. Is that a bee sting? Your hand's swollen twice its size."

Quinn leaned forward to hear better.

"It's two hornet stings, Mrs. Dick. Mr. Shadwell and I surprised a nest of them this morning."

"Did Miss Ramona put Dead Sea mud on you? I know she bought a bag of it from the door-to-door salesman."

"Oh, sure, she put mud on it when it happened. That's why I smell like pond weeds." Justin laughed, and goosebumps rose on Quinn's arms.

Justin's laugh could charm hummingbirds better than nectar in a cup, Quinn thought as she ran upstairs, remembering one of Beau John's enchanted stories.

She stopped suddenly, bent over with a pain she couldn't understand. Where was he? Where was her father?

Quinn and Grandma had the last of the laundry out by one o'clock. They were sitting on the front porch sipping lemonade when Auntie Sis returned home, red-faced and exasperated.

"Did you get the job?" Grandma asked as Auntie Sis climbed the steps.

"I did not," Auntie Sis said. She sat down beside Grandma and removed her hat. Her damp hair stuck to her forehead in small curls. "I waited nearly two hours to see that man — and standing up the whole time, too! I thought my back would break. And it was so hot! And in the end, that insufferable man told me he'd never hire anybody as old as I am because his customers want to see a perky girl maybe sixteen or seventeen behind the counter. And so he hired one."

"Sakes," Grandma muttered, scowling, as she got to her feet. "Well, I'm sorry, lovey. You look exhausted. I'll go in and fix you a nice lunch. I've got a cucumber and Quinn brought lettuce in from the garden. And you'll need good hot tea."

"I'm too tired to change clothes," Auntie Sis complained. "But I've got to save this dress for another job interview, and who knows when that might come up?"

Groaning, she stood up and went inside. Quinn sipped lemonade and stared into space. Everything depended on money. No matter what else seemed important, eventually money was involved. Had she been blind to that before?

Child. She was a child. Amy had been right. Beau

John risked everything — even jail! — so that he could earn money for the family. Amy quit school. Auntie Sis endured humiliation. Uncle Dick was heaven-knew-where, standing in another long line, hoping he would be chosen. Grandma was too old to work and Mama was too sick. And Feep was still in grade school.

Across the street, Betty Caster came out her front door and stretched out on the porch swing. She wore a skimpy sleeveless dress, and her hair was covered with a turban. When she saw Quinn, she waved lazily.

Quinn stood up abruptly and hurried across the street. Betty, lounging, watched her indifferently until Quinn pushed open the Casters' gate. Then Betty sat up abruptly. She and Quinn weren't friends. Quinn had never gone across the street to see her before.

Quinn climbed the steps and stood before Betty. Now that she was there, her tongue seemed to have stuck to the roof of her mouth.

"How are you?" Betty asked. Quinn noticed for the first time that Betty was smoking a cigarette.

"Beau John didn't come home Saturday night," Quinn said.

Betty's penciled eyebrows rose. "He didn't?" she asked, but she sounded as if she already knew.

"We haven't heard anything from him. He's never been this late before."

Betty leaned back again and drew hard on her cigarette. "I'm sorry to hear that. I'm sure you count on having him home on Sundays."

Quinn took a step closer. "You said something the other night about him. That he knew Mike's friends."

"Sure," Betty said. "So?"

Quinn swallowed hard. "Does that mean that they might know where Beau John works?"

She had Betty's interest now. Betty didn't even blink.

"How would I know what they know?" the young woman countered cautiously.

"Have you heard where Beau John works?" Quinn asked.

Betty blinked. "Where would I hear something like that?"

Quinn bit her lip. "The other night, you said things that sounded as if Beau John and Mike knew the same people, maybe even worked . . ." She couldn't go on. She couldn't give Betty even a hint about the conversation Beau John had with the stranger. But everyone was aware of Mike's association with gangsters. And gangsters had something to do with the smugglers and rumrunners who brought Canadian whiskey into the country.

And Betty wasn't about to admit to knowledge that could get her in trouble.

"Look," Quinn said. "I need to find my father, but I

don't know where to look. If you were in my place — if you needed to find someone — where would you start?"

Betty looked away and inhaled smoke deeply. Seconds ticked by. Finally, without looking at Quinn, she said, "I'd ask Mike."

Hope surged through Quinn. "Would you? Would you ask him for me?"

Betty shook her head and laughed bitterly. "Are you crazy? Mike thinks I'm deaf and blind, and I plan on keeping it that way."

Quinn pressed her fingers against her mouth for a moment, then said, "Okay. I'll ask him. Where can I find him?"

Betty studied her fingernails for a long time before she spoke. "You know Jules' Card Room across the bridge?"

Of course she knew the card room. It and the bridge figured in more than one of her nightmares. "Mike hangs out there?"

"Sometimes," Betty said. She looked disgusted. "When he's there, he's in the back room."

"Where they sell liquor," Quinn said. She began shaking her head.

"Well, I didn't mean for you to go *in* there!" Betty exclaimed.

"Then what?" Quinn asked. "How can I talk to him?"

"Ask one of the men up front to go get him," Betty said with a great show of patience.

"Ask one of the men on the sidewalk?" Quinn exclaimed.

"No, no, no," Betty said. "Heavens. They only hang around. They don't *know* anything. Stand in the doorway and ask one of the men at the card tables to tell Mike you want to talk to him. He'll go in the back and get him. Maybe."

"Thanks," Quinn said. She turned to leave.

"I hope you find your dad," Betty said. "He's a nice man."

"Yes. Thank you." She studied Betty's face for a moment. Had she seen a flicker of unease in those doll-like eyes?

She was imagining things.

Quinn ran back across the street and reached the top of her own porch steps just as Grandma and Auntie Sis came out, with Mama right behind them.

"Mama!" Quinn exclaimed guiltily. She had thought her mother was still resting in her room.

"I feel ashamed of myself, staying in bed half the day," Mama said. She looked better. The color was back in her face.

"You ladies sit right down," Grandma said. "I've got a whole tray of sandwiches here, and I'll bring the tea out in a second."

"I hope Feep doesn't decide to come roaring home

now," Auntie Sis said as she reached for one of the dainty cucumber sandwiches. "This pretty little lunch is not for men."

Quinn waited until Grandma brought out the tea before she asked if anyone needed anything from the store.

"Bless your heart," Grandma said. "I'll write you out a list."

"You should leave soon," Mama said. "The day's only going to get hotter and hotter."

"I'll go now," Quinn said. "Can I have that list, Grandma?"

"Sure. And don't forget to stop by and tell Miss Clotilde yes or no about Wednesday."

"I won't forget," Quinn said, although she had. Earning small amounts of money lettering cards seemed so frivolous at a time like this.

Shortly, she had the list and the coin purse, so she crossed the street to the Dallas cottage, wound her way through the laundry hanging from the tangle of lines, and knocked on the back screen door.

Justin answered, surprising her. "Hey," he said. "Hey, Quinn. What's up?"

"I came to tell Miss Clotilde that I'll be here Wednesday morning," Quinn said. She saw Justin's swollen hand and winced. "Gosh, your hand looks terrible."

"I was just about to mix up another batch of my

aunt's mud," Justin said, laughing a little. "I know it sounds foolish, but it really helps."

Miss Clotilde came up behind him and greeted Quinn. "I heard you tell Justin that you'd be here Wednesday. That's good, because I went downtown this morning and got us a job lettering birthday invitations and the envelopes, too."

Quinn was impressed. "How many? How long do we have?"

"Fifty, and we'll have until next week, so we don't need to worry."

"You ladies are getting to be giants of industry," Justin said. He had crossed to the sink and was stirring something in a pot with a wooden spoon.

"Here, let me do that," Miss Clotilde said. She pushed him aside. "Go out back and get Mr. Shadwell. I'll slap some fresh mud on him, too. He got more stings than you did."

"I'll ask him, but I can't guarantee he'll come in," Justin said. He held open the screen door. "You leaving or staying, Quinn?"

"Leaving," she said. She thought he looked disappointed. "I've got some errands."

"Sure," Justin said. "See you later."

"Quinn, you heard anything from Beau John yet?" Miss Clotilde asked.

"No. I hoped we'd get a letter but we didn't."

"There'll be another delivery this afternoon," Miss Clotilde said. "Keep your fingers crossed."

But Quinn had resigned herself to seeing the mailman pass them by again.

The sun seemed hotter already. Quinn walked past Donna's house, wishing she was home instead of downtown in the newspaper office. Maybe she'd come out to say something. Then, when Donna did appear on the porch, her hair wrapped in a towel, Quinn was almost speechless.

"Are you going to the store?" Donna called out. "Can you wait a few minutes while I comb out my hair? I'll come, too."

"I'm in a hurry," Quinn said. She couldn't have Donna with her when she stopped off at the card room. But she didn't want another day to pass without talking to the girl who had been her best friend all her life. Somehow they had to keep in touch, even though Donna had changed her life. "What are you doing home? I thought you started work today."

"I went in this morning," Donna called out. "The person who was supposed to teach me my job left at noon, so they told me to come back tomorrow morning. Will you stop by on your way home?"

"I'll try," Quinn said. She waved and hurried away quickly, to make up for the lost time.

She would stop at the grocery store after she talked

to Mike. But first, she must conquer her fear of going over the bridge alone.

In the hot sunlight, the wooden bridge smelled of creosote, and it trembled a little under her light feet. She hated it. It spanned the railroad tracks like a giant, malformed spider. Below, on one side, Hooverville lay huddled next to the dirt bank, its tin and plywood roofs baking in the sun. Here and there, a short line of ragged laundry connected two or more of the shacks. A cook fire smouldered sullenly at one end. An odorous outhouse leaned drunkenly beside the bank at the other end. An old man crossing Hooverville's dirt path looked up, saw Quinn staring over the railing, and looked away as if ashamed to be seen there.

She walked on, her heels clattering on the blackened planks. Two locomotives idled on the tracks below. She had seen them before she started across the bridge, and they represented her greatest dread. Once long before, when she had been very small, she and Mama had been halfway across the bridge when an engine released a great blast of steam and it spurted upward, hissing viciously, and shot past the railing before it finally dissipated harmlessly above them. She had screamed in terror, and once again she felt the utter helplessness she had felt that day, when the black iron monster on the tracks, hideous as any dragon, had threatened her.

She hurried a little faster.

Think ahead, she told herself. Plan what you'll say to Mike.

The engines were directly below her, chuffing a little, smelling of coal smoke.

Oh please, oh please, oh please.

She ran the last few feet, almost flying over the bridge planks, and when she reached the sidewalk, she stopped and looked back. A thin dribble of smoke crept up from the engines.

Maybe they would be gone when she came back.

The small shopping district lay ahead. She could see the card room sign hanging out over the sidewalk, and under it, close to the gutter, half a dozen men stood talking and smoking together.

I can do this, Quinn told herself. But her walk slowed. Still, she reached the men faster than she expected.

She stopped. They looked curiously at her.

She turned toward the doorway that stood open between two painted-over windows. The men at the curb muttered among themselves, speaking in lower voices now.

She crossed the threshold of the card room and stopped.

Immediately all the men at the tables in the room looked up. One man, an old fellow with tightly curled white hair, said, "You don't want anything in here, missy."

Quinn stood her ground, but she could hear her heart beat in her ears. "I'd like to speak to Mike, please," she said.

"No Mike here," the old man said. Another man snickered.

Quinn's face burned. "I'd like to speak to Mike, please," she repeated. "Mike O'Hara."

She waited while they stared at her, then at each other. One man in the back, who sat near a closed door, got to his feet and opened the door.

"Anybody named Mike O'Hara back here?" he called out, and then he laughed.

"Who wants to know?" Quinn heard someone say.

The man turned around and looked at her for a long moment. Then he said to the voice inside, "A skinny kid with a long braid wants to know."

Mike appeared in the doorway, in rolled-up shirtsleeves, with his tie hanging loose around his neck. He gawked at Quinn in astonishment.

"Jeez, it's Beau John's kid," he said.

Everyone in the card room stared at Quinn.

Mike hurried across the room, rolling down his sleeves as if his bare wrists betrayed him somehow. He took her arm when he reached her and led her twenty feet down the sidewalk, close to the curtained window of the dentist's office.

"What are you doing here?" Mike whispered, looking back over his shoulder. "What's the big idea, coming here and asking for me?"

"Where's Beau John?" Quinn asked. "He didn't come home Saturday."

She could tell from his expression that he wasn't surprised. But he said, "How in hell should I know where your old man is?"

This was going to be the hard part. "He said if I needed him, I could ask you," she lied. "He said, 'Mike can find me and get a message to me.' I need to send him a message, so where is he?"

Mike was astonished first, and then outraged. "Don't kid me, kid. I don't know where Beau John is, so I can't get a message to him."

"Then who can?" Quinn persisted quickly. She was afraid she would lose him, afraid he would turn away and return to the dingy card room where she was so unwelcome. "Tell me who knows where he is. You and Beau John know the same people. Help me find him. He'd want you to."

Mike stared straight at her. His eyes were a clear, topaz blue, as innocent as Feep's.

"Please, Mike," she whispered.

He stared a moment more, then shook his head as if to rid himself of a fly. "Jeez, Beau John's kid," he said to no one. He bent over her suddenly. "Go ask Double D. He worked with your dad a couple of times, and he showed up alone last Friday. He'll know something, but I can't promise he'll be willing to tell you anything. He's new around here."

"Where is he? Where can I find this Double D?"

"He's using a shack in Hooverville," Mike said. "I don't know which one. Don't go there by yourself."

With that, Mike broke away from her and almost ran back to the card room. The men on the sidewalk stared at Quinn.

"Beau John's kid," someone whispered. She saw curiosity in their faces.

She crossed the street and walked to the grocery store, her ears ringing, heart thudding. What could she do? Go to Hooverville alone?

Beau John, where are you?

She looked up once before she ducked into the store. The pitiless sky burned a hard blue overhead, and there was no answer and no relief for her there.

Ten

She had to deal with the bridge again, only this time she carried two sacks of groceries, so running across it was out of the question. One train engine was still there, dribbling smoke, waiting. The bridge shook under her feet. The sun's heat felt almost liquid, burning her bare head. The smell of creosote was overwhelming.

Under the far side of the bridge, dusty Hooverville was silent. In one of those sagging huts, there was a man called Double D, and Quinn would have to talk to him.

But she would have to return home first. The women in the house expected her, and if she was late, they'd wonder and ask their mild questions, expecting a tale of gossip exchanged with a neighbor or an amazing sight. What excuse could she give them so that they wouldn't care that she went back out again so soon?

She could blame it all on Donna. She'd tell them Donna wanted her to stop by.

But what if Donna saw her hurrying up the street again and wanted to go along?

Quinn would use the street that ran behind the Dallas cottage and Donna's house. It was a block out of the way, but Donna wouldn't see her there. Her back fence was too high.

As soon as Quinn came into the kitchen, Grandma demanded that she sit down. "Your face is red," Grandma said. "You look exhausted. Lookie here, I'll fix you a cold compress for your forehead, and you have a good rest in here with us."

Auntie Sis took the groceries out of Quinn's arms and shook her head. "Did you run back? We weren't in that much of a hurry for these odds and ends."

"I didn't run, but it's hot out there," Quinn said. She pushed away the cloth Grandma had wrung out in cold water. "Honestly, Grandma, I don't need it. I'm going over to Donna's. She got off work early and I want to hear all about everything."

"Early on her first day?" Mama said as she came into the kitchen. "Is everything all right with her job?"

"Sure, sure," Quinn said. "But I want to hear the news, so I'm going over there now. I'll see you all . . ."

Uncle Dick came in, interrupting her. He, too, was flushed from the heat. And he looked upset.

"Oh, my," Auntie Sis said as soon as she saw him. "I don't even need to ask how your luck was."

"Luck? I don't think what happened to me had anything to do with luck." Uncle Dick sat down at the table and accepted the glass of water Mama handed him. "Well, ladies, it turned out that practically everybody in the state was there looking for work, but the smelter was only hiring five temporary workers and the money wouldn't have paid for my gas driving back and forth to Tacoma. But I did meet a fellow who said he thought there might be some cannery work up north, so I believe I'll look into that tomorrow first thing."

"Somewhere around where Beau John is working?" Mama asked as she refilled Uncle Dick's glass.

"Wouldn't that be wonderful?" Uncle Dick asked, pleased at the thought. "We could make the drive together." But then he laughed. "No, it wouldn't be wonderful. Both of us would be gone for days at a time. I tell you, times are pretty bad when a man is glad to have the hardest kind of work and be away from his family all the time." He took a deep gulp from the glass and set it down. "Did you get a letter from Beau John? I was hoping all day you would."

"No, nothing yet," Mama said. "But I don't believe the afternoon mail has come."

A momentary hope, bright as a falling star, brought a smile to Quinn's face. Maybe there would be a letter.

"I saw the mailman ten minutes ago," Grandma said. "He walked right on by, so we won't be hearing today."

Instant gloom fell on the room, and Quinn cleared

her throat. "Well, I'll go on over to Donna's for a while," she said vaguely, concerned about getting away.

"Don't you get any ideas about quitting school the way she did," Mama said sharply. "Losing one of my girls to hard times is enough."

Quinn stopped and turned around. "Mama, you know very well that Amy was tired of school and wanted to work. Most of the people in her class left before she did. That's just how it is these days."

"But you won't leave," Mama said. "What would I tell your father?"

The mention of Beau John reminded Quinn that she didn't have much time. "You won't have to tell him anything, Mama," she said. "I'm only going over to see how Donna likes her job. Probably she hates it."

She left quickly before Mama could call her back with another warning. She hoped that no one was watching out the kitchen window, because she turned up the gravel side road instead of down.

Don't look back, she told herself. If someone is watching and asks about it, I'll tell them I wanted to see if Justin had started on the yellow apple trees yet.

But that was silly. They didn't ripen until the end of the month. In between picking peaches and the yellow apples, he'd begin the big task of cutting the orchard grass with a sickle.

As she turned the corner at the back of the Dallas land, she caught a glimpse of Justin between trees. His back was turned to her. She hurried a little faster, passing Mr. Shadwell's one-room shack. Usually he spent the afternoons dozing in a chair by his door, but the chair was empty. Quinn hurried on.

Next she came to the tall fence that belonged to Donna's family, and then a long, straggling picket fence that wandered to the end of the block. Safely out of sight now, Quinn turned to the main street that led to the bridge.

But she wouldn't be crossing the bridge this time. There was a well-worn trail that led into a strip of dusty maple trees hanging over the edge of the ravine. She knew its location — every youngster on Tapestry Hill knew. Once, in a daring mood, she and Donna had walked along the trail as far as the steep steps cut into the side of the ravine. The steps led down to Hooverville.

In spite of the heat, half the neighborhood was out on the sidewalk. Quinn said hello a dozen times on her way to the bridge. Twice women asked her if her family had heard the latest news about Pete DePiano — the sick child had taken a turn for the worse.

Everyone asked about Beau John.

Quinn bit her lip and walked on. She should plan what she would say to this man called Double D. All her life, she'd had a tendency to stammer if she was nervous. She'd better not stammer this time. She must sound brave.

For the first time, Hooverville appeared thoroughly menacing to her. Beau John had been there at least once. When the railroad people had wanted to force out the poor souls who lived in the shacks, Beau John and half a dozen other men from the hill went downtown to the railroad office and spoke up for the place. If those impoverished men couldn't live there, then where would they go? They weren't out of work because they were lazy. There were no jobs. No one had expected Beau John and his friends to be successful, but they were. Beau John could work magic sometimes. That particular shantytown remained, even while others, both in Seattle and across the country, were deliberately destroyed when more prosperous citizens complained.

She passed four grade school girls playing hopscotch. Suddenly she remembered the flat green rock Beau John had given her when she was young enough for the game. She and Donna and the other girls their age in the neighborhood always played on the corner in front of the Wagners' house, and Quinn kept her special hopscotch rock safe in a secret niche in the stonework around their steps. It must still be there, although she hadn't taken it out in two years.

I wish I was still that young, she thought fiercely.

Amy knew she went up to the attic to play with the dolls? That was embarrassing. But the dolls were so sweet. Miss Clotilde had told her once about a rich woman's doll collection that she had seen when she went to the woman's house to deliver a special order of party invitations. There was a whole room of glass cases filled with dolls with long hair and fluffy petticoats. If a woman could play with dolls, then surely it was all right if Quinn did. What would Beau John say about it? Should she tell him — when she saw him again?

If she saw him again.

She was nearing the terrible old bridge. Forty feet to the right, the trail was visible under the dusty maples. Quinn turned toward it. But out of the corner of her eye, she saw a figure duck behind a telephone pole.

She whirled around, gasping.

Mr. Shadwell!

"Mr. Shadwell, what do you want?" she called out to him.

He hesitated a moment, then walked toward her. When he reached her, he pointed toward the trail and sketched a question mark in the air. Then he shook his head hard. Clearly he was warning her.

She didn't know what to do. He never spoke, but he wouldn't have any difficulty in telling her family where she'd gone.

"Look," she said. "I've got to go down there to find someone. It's . . ."

Mr. Shadwell shook his head again.

"It's important, Mr. Shadwell. I have to do this."

He shook his head.

This was terrible! "Mr. Shadwell, you know Beau

John didn't come home Saturday the way he was supposed to."

Mr. Shadwell nodded.

"There's supposed to be a man in Hooverville who knows where he is. I've got to find him."

Mr. Shadwell blinked, paused, and then touched his chest and pointed to the trail.

He wants to go with me, Quinn thought, dizzy with relief. Maybe this could work. Maybe his presence would keep her safe and afterward he wouldn't tell anyone.

"Do you promise not to tell anyone?" she asked.

He shook his head. He wouldn't promise.

Now what?

Mr. Shadwell touched her arm and cocked his head at the trail. He touched his chest again and pointed toward Hooverville.

She didn't have a choice. "All right," she said. "Just remember we're doing this for Beau John, and before you tell anybody anything, think of what it might do to Beau John if people knew . . . if . . ." She broke off, not even sure what she meant.

He nodded and shuffled around her, taking the lead. He looked back only once to see if she followed.

When they stepped into the woods, they were out of sight of people who might pass on the bridge. Mr. Shadwell moved faster now, and he seemed to be familiar with the trail. When they reached the place where steps had been cut into the bank, Mr. Shadwell started down without hesitating.

The steps were worn by the many feet that had climbed up and down. In some places, where the steps had been worn into a slope, Mr. Shadwell's shoes slipped dangerously, and Quinn held her breath. He was old and crippled. What would she do if he fell and hurt himself? This was a mistake.

When they reached the bottom at last, Quinn saw that Hooverville, which looked nearly deserted from the bridge, was actually crowded. Two dozen men peered at them from the shady sides of their shacks, from doorways, from a lean-to made of canvas, from what appeared to be the wooden crate that had once contained a piano. No one made a threatening gesture or sound, but Quinn was terrified.

Mr. Shadwell approached the nearest man, who seemed to recognize him. At least, he greeted the old fellow with a nod and a weary smile.

Mr. Shadwell touched his chest with one finger and then turned to point at Quinn.

"The young lady's your friend," the man said.

Mr. Shadwell nodded, and then he stepped aside and made a gesture as if ushering Quinn forward.

She took a step.

"I'm looking for someone called Double D," she said. Her voice shook and she stammered.

The man stared but said nothing.

Mr. Shadwell touched her arm. When she looked at him, he raised one hand over his head, as if measuring something. When she didn't understand, he pointed at her, and then he raised his hand over his head again, measuring the air.

Someone tall?

Beau John?

She whirled around to the man. "I'm Beau John's daughter," she blurted, hoping she was doing the right thing. "He didn't come home when he should have, and someone told me that Double D might know where he is."

"You're Beau John's kid?" the man asked. He got to his feet immediately. The men nearest to them got up, too, and gathered around. Quinn heard, "Beau John," over and over.

The first man brushed at his soiled shirt helplessly. "I'm ashamed that you found me like this," he said. He gestured to the box he'd been sitting on. "Do you want to sit down? I'm sorry I don't have anything to offer you except water and bread."

Quinn was overwhelmed with embarrassment and guilt. She had been afraid of these poor men who seemed to know her father well. She didn't want to hurt them but she didn't have time to accept even the smallest gesture of hospitality. "Thank you, but I only want to find this man called Double D. Do you know where he is?"

"Come this way," the man said, and the other men made room for them to walk between them. "He's pretty sick — has been ever since he got here. But he — well, I'll let him tell you what he knows."

He ducked in a low doorway in a shack made of plywood and spoke to someone in the dark. "D, here's Beau John's daughter."

Quinn heard a groan and a scrabbling sound, and then a man near her father's age hobbled to the doorway. His left foot was covered with a soiled bandage, and the left side of his face was scraped raw and scabbed over. He smiled when he saw Quinn, and winced from the pain the smile had cost him.

"How do, miss? I see your pa in you. You've got his eyes and mouth. Are you Amy or Quinn?"

"Quinn," she said. His appearance alarmed her. "Is my father all right?"

The man's gaze shifted between her and the man who had led her to his shack. When he looked back at her, she saw that his expression was guarded now.

"I haven't seen your father since Thursday," he said. He hobbled to a wooden box and sat down. "Excuse me, miss, but I can't stand up very long." He looked up at her. "We were stopped by the Federal cops Thursday night right after we picked up a load from a boat on the beach."

She suddenly realized what he was talking about. It was a load of *whiskey!* Now Quinn knew that all her suspicions about the conversation she'd overheard were true. There was no way around it, no other explanation for it. Her father was part of a group of smugglers.

"What happened?" Quinn asked. Her mouth was dry.

"We got forced off a dirt road," Double D said. "I was driving. I jumped out and took off running, and I know your father did, too. I looked for Beau John as best I could, but I was hurt and I needed to find a place to hide in the woods."

Quinn pressed her fingers to her mouth for a moment. "Is he alive?" she asked.

"Oh, I'm sure of it," the man said heartily. "Certainly he's alive! But the woods are heavy there, and it was dark, and I didn't dare yell for him because there's no telling who might have been listening. Those Federal cops don't like to give up, and they can't be bought, either. We had to be careful. I made my way to the main road by morning, and I expected to see Beau John somewhere on that road, but I didn't. I got a ride that took me most of the way here. I've asked everybody who's come and gone since then if they've seen or heard about him, but so far nobody knows anything."

Quinn's disappointment was so great that she had trouble keeping tears out of her eyes. "Do you know anybody who might know something?" she asked.

"There was a man who came to see Beau John more than a week ago. I overheard them talking. The man seemed to know everything about what Beau John was doing. Maybe he was the one who hired Beau John. Do you know who that could have been?"

The man shook his head. "The man who owned the truck is the one who hired me, and he never comes to Seattle."

"But couldn't you get in touch with him and see if he knows where my father is?" Quinn persisted.

"Miss, I don't know how to get hold of him," the man said. "When he wanted me, he came looking for me. Every couple of days he'd show up at this boarding house where I was staying, and he'd turn the truck over to me and tell me where and when to pick up the crates the boats left on the beach and where to deliver them. Beau John was rooming with a family, but I don't know who they were or where they were. He was always waiting at the pickup place with the cash we'd need to pay off the local cops if they stopped us. He was what they called a Bookkeeper. I was the driver. I always let him off at the same place because his car would be somewhere around. He had to give back the payoff money — you bet your life he had to give it back or account for what we used like when the local boys bothered us a couple of times. But I don't know who his contact is, and he didn't tell. That's how this business is. You only learn what you have to know."

Quinn had to ask a hard question now. "Could my father be in jail?"

"No, no," the man said hastily. "Don't you worry about that. The ones who hired us are only small potatoes, and nothing much happens to them. I never was so surprised in my life as I was when I realized it was Federal boys after us, not the county fellows who are pretty friendly."

But of course she would worry. If Beau John had been caught, would he tell anyone where his family was? She had no idea what happened when someone was arrested.

Mr. Shadwell seemed depressed by the news they'd been given, and Quinn was, too. There was no point in prolonging the conversation. The man was ill, and he didn't know anything that could help them. Quinn thanked him and began picking her way back along the dirt path that wound between the shacks.

A tall, thin man in soiled overalls stepped in front of her and stopped her. "Tell your people he'd be a fool to go into a town now to mail a letter or send a telegram," the man whispered. "The Federal cops won't be the only ones looking for him. If he's carrying cash for a payoff, it's gangster money, and nobody's safe with gangster money until it's back where it belongs. After that, your family will hear from him."

The man backed away immediately, but Quinn said, "Who are you? How do you know this?"

The man didn't answer, but vanished behind a row of shacks.

Mr. Shadwell gave her a gentle shove, and when she turned to look at him, he scowled, put one finger over his lips, and then pointed ahead.

He wanted her to stop talking and hurry. What was going on? Who was the man who had spoken to her?

They were halfway up the dirt steps in the hillside when Quinn, who was leading, stopped and faced Mr. Shadwell.

"Do you know who that man was? The one who told me Beau John isn't safe until he returns the payoff money?"

Mr. Shadwell scowled darkly, then formed a circle with his fingers and held it against his chest.

"His heart? Something about his heart?"

Mr. Shadwell shook his head. He formed the circle again and smacked it against his chest. Then he formed his hand to look like Feep's when he was playing cops and robbers without a toy gun.

"The man's a policeman?" Quinn gasped.

Mr. Shadwell shook his head, nodded it, and shook it again, then made a gesture as if saying goodbye.

"He was one but now he isn't?" Quinn asked.

Mr. Shadwell nodded once and shoved her gently again, gesturing her to go! Go!

Was there anything Mr. Shadwell didn't know?

He didn't know where Beau John was.

Quinn began climbing again, and reached the top long before Mr. Shadwell. She stopped to wait for him, and she stared down into Hooverville, marveling at the tangled secrets it held.

"I hope you two know what you're doing," Justin said.

Quinn swung around and nearly lost her balance. "Justin!"

"Did you think you were invisible, sneaking around in back of my aunts' place?" Justin asked. "I saw you first and then Mr. Shadwell, and I knew I'd better tag along and make sure the two of you didn't get into some kind of trouble you couldn't solve. For Pete's sake, what were you doing down in that shantytown?"

"Never mind," Quinn said. She edged around him and hurried along the trail.

He was right behind her. "Were you looking for your father? Why would he stay down there when he's so close to home?"

"It's none of your business," Quinn said.

"Does your mother know you went down there?"

Quinn whirled around. "Don't you say one word to Mama!" she cried. "She's sick, and she doesn't need anything more to worry about."

"Then why are you doing things that would worry

her?" Justin nagged. "If you aren't looking for Beau John, what are you doing?"

Mr. Shadwell grabbed Justin before the boy saw him. He jerked him around and scowled.

Justin shook his arm loose. "Mr. Shadwell, you shouldn't have gone there, either. What would my aunts say if they find out?"

Mr. Shadwell shook his head, pushed him aside, and started home.

"You can't say anything to anybody," Quinn told Justin. "Please. I was trying to find out something about my father — there's a man in Hooverville who knows him — but he doesn't know where he is, either."

"You should have told your family and let your uncle go down there," Justin argued.

"No, I couldn't, and never mind why," Quinn said. If she had told Uncle Dick about Double D, he'd want to know how such a man knew Beau John. How could she tell Uncle Dick that Beau John helped support him by smuggling illegal whiskey into the country?

No one must find out anything bad about Beau John! This had to be her secret, forever. Everyone loved him. How would they feel if they learned that he was a criminal?

Justin grabbed her hand suddenly, surprising her. "Don't do anything like this again," he said.

She snatched back her hand. "I won't," she said.

If the stranger in Hooverville was right, how long would it take for Beau John to return the money and send them a message?

The three of them walked home single file, as if they were strangers. Beau John's secrets had made them so.

Eleven

Quinn refused to walk down the main street, but instead hurried along the road that ran behind the Dallas cottage. Justin and Mr. Shadwell followed her as she hoped they would. There was no point in alerting Donna or anyone else that something strange was going on with the Wagner family.

She heard Feep bawling as she pushed open the back gate, and she broke into a run, expecting the worst. Something had happened to Beau John and the family knew!

Feep danced in a furious circle on the kitchen floor, his fists clenched, his face red with rage. Grandma and Auntie Sis stood open-mouthed at the stove. Mama wiped her hands on a blue-checked towel and reached out for her boy.

At that moment, Uncle Dick tore open the basement door and popped into the kitchen, holding a short length of pipe. "What!" he roared as he looked around wildly. "Who? What?"

"Mama!" Quinn yelled over Feep's shrieks. "What's wrong?"

Auntie Sis unceremoniously clapped her hand over Feep's mouth and said loudly, "I'll give you a lump of brown sugar if you stop screaming!"

Feep nodded, and when she took her hand away, he was silent.

"What the hell is going on?" Uncle Dick cried. "I thought there was bloody murder going on up here, and I came prepared." He shook the pipe to demonstrate.

"It has something to do with Elizabetta," Mama began.

Feep crammed the brown sugar into his mouth and talked around it. "That bad old woman caught us when we were putting our get-well cards for Pete in the crack in their door and she slapped Monkey Jackson and then she tore up the card I made and threw it at me." He wiped the sugar from his mouth on the back of his hand and sat down triumphantly.

Mama leaned over him. "Calm down, calm down. You can make another card."

"But she won't let Pete have it!" Feep shouted. "She said my card had a curse on it and Pete would die if he touched it."

"Oh, lawks, but that old woman is crazy," Auntie Sis grumbled. "Feep, you're smarter than that. She's an evil, nasty old woman, and you're a wonderful little boy, to make a card for a child you didn't even like very much."

"Because he stole my aggie," Feep said, wiping his nose on the back of his hand. "My best aggie that didn't have any chips in it, either."

"Forget that aggie," Uncle Dick said. "I'll buy you another myself. But you'd better stay away from the DePiano house before something worse happens to you."

"Monkey's mother has a temper and a half," Mama mused. "I wonder how she'll take it that Elizabetta hit him."

"Oh, she'll scorch the air," Grandma said with satisfaction.

"DePiano will have to do something with that old woman one of these days," Uncle Dick said.

Amy came in, pulling off her hat. "Goodness, it's getting muggy out there. I saw storm clouds building up in the west. Oh, dinner smells good. Is that ham, Auntie Sis?" She stopped talking abruptly and looked around. "What's wrong?"

"Elizabetta scared Feep again," Grandma said briskly. She repeated the story while Amy removed her hat and gloves.

Amy kissed Feep's forehead, then turned and said to Grandma, "I told Carl about awful old Elizabetta, and he said we — the people in the neighborhood — can require the family to have her examined by a judge and a doctor, and if she's found to be crazy — and we know she is — they'll put her away in a hospital."

"Let's do it!" Feep cried. "Let's do that today!"

"Let's leave that to your father when he gets home," Mama told him as she set the butter on the table. "I think we're about ready, everybody. Wash your hands, Feep. Amy, do you want to run upstairs and change out of your office dress? Hurry up, child."

Amy clattered away in her high heels and Quinn helped Feep at the sink. Uncle Dick sat down and flapped his napkin into his lap. "We need another good rain before we start into the dog days."

"I imagine Justin appreciates a little cooling off," Auntie Sis said. "Miss Ramona told me today that he's biding time now, waiting for more apples to turn ripe."

"He's got his work cut out for him over there, anyway," Uncle Dick said. "The place is falling down. Beau John was thinking about putting together a neighborhood party and doing a few things for the old ladies before winter gets here."

Quinn's eyes suddenly filled with tears. She couldn't help it. But she didn't turn away from her family quickly enough, because everyone saw that she was crying.

"Ah, honey, don't you worry about your dad," Auntie Sis said. "Your uncle's right. Beau John found some extra work and that's what's delayed him."

Mama patted Quinn's shoulder. "If something had happened to him, we'd have heard. It's not as if he's in some foreign country and nobody knows his name or speaks his language. If he'd been hurt, he'd have asked somebody to get in touch with us right away."

Amy was back, tying the narrow sash of a cotton dress snugly around her waist. "Don't worry, Quinn. Beau John could show up any time. He's fine — and so are we! Carl thinks our family is wonderful, and he keeps asking what he can do to help us. See? Beau John's away, but we aren't alone. We've got Uncle Dick and even Carl now."

Uncle Dick nodded. "Beau John will like him."

"I know," Amy said, smiling.

Quinn tried to eat, but the food stuck in her throat. Her family was like a flock of children, so trusting and innocent. They believed what Beau John had told them, that the world was a good place.

After dinner, she helped clear the table, and then, when she was alone, she climbed all the stairs to the attic, pushed open the door, and pulled the string that turned on the single bulb.

The attic was hot and dusty, but there was a round window at one end that opened on a hinge, and Quinn pushed it ajar. She looked down on the Dallas cottage, snuggled in among the fruit trees, surrounded by a wobbly old fence. Two dogs farther up the street barked at a boy on a bicycle.

The air smelled dusty and heavy, and there was no wind. Quinn left the window and opened the old green tin trunk in the corner.

There were the dolls, all of hers and all of Amy's. There were even two of the dolls Mama had played with when she was a girl, and an old, fragile glass doll that belonged to Grandma. Quinn took them out carefully, one by one, and arranged them around her on the floor. There was one, her favorite, that she held in her lap and rocked gently. She called the doll Rachel, and whispered her name as she rocked. The doll's hair was long and dark, like Quinn's, and its eyes were like Quinn's.

"What am I going to do?" she whispered to Rachel as she rocked her. "Who can I talk to?"

Beau John had told her once that dolls always hear when their owners speak to them. "Rachel," she whispered against the doll's face. "Where's our Beau John?"

The wild storm broke during the night, waking both Quinn and Amy.

"Is the window open?" Amy asked in the dark. "Heavens! It is! And the floor's wet, too. Quinn, get a towel."

Quinn heard the window slam as she swung her feet out of bed. She fumbled to turn the light on, brought a towel from the bathroom, and dropped it on the puddle below the window.

Amy peered at her alarm clock. "The alarm's going off in another twenty minutes! Why don't things like this happen when there's still time to fall back to sleep?"

Quinn sopped up the water on the floor and carried the towel back to the bathroom. The house seemed cold. She jumped into bed gratefully and pulled the blankets up to her chin.

Amy turned out the light and was silent for a moment. Then she said, "Quinn, did Dad ever talk about his job to you?"

Quinn's stomach seemed to tie into a knot. "Not much, no. He told me about things that happened around the dock. The dancing dog. Things like that."

Amy sighed. "I don't think I ever understood exactly what he does."

Quinn cleared her throat. "He unloads baggage and cargo from passenger boats that stop there. He told us about the big hotel, remember? All the people who come there wearing beautiful clothes?"

"Sometimes it makes me angry when I think that there are still people rich enough to take vacations and stay at luxury hotels when the rest of the country is so poor." Surprised, Quinn could hear her sister punching her pillow.

"Beau John told us that we ought to be glad there are people like that," Quinn said.

"He was talking about the rich people we read about

in the papers, who are always getting into trouble and being divorced and fighting over their children's custody," Amy said. "He said we ought to be glad because their lives are so glamorous that they entertain us the way the movies do."

"Beau John thinks we ought to be glad that *everybody* was born," Quinn said.

"I wonder where he is," Amy said. "I wish I knew for certain. I can't help worrying a little, but I don't want Mama to know."

"He's fine," Quinn said. She stirred restlessly and turned over. "He's fine."

Neither of them went back to sleep.

The rain was over by the time Amy left for work. Uncle Dick, always hopeful, left a few minutes later to chase down the rumor of another job.

Feep had been cranky since he sat down for breakfast, and his mood grew worse when Mama told him she wanted him to stay away from Monkey's house.

"You're always getting in trouble when you play with him," Mama said. "And he's disrespectful. I wouldn't be surprised if he grew up to be a crook. Pick somebody else. Why don't you play with Jackie Sumner? He's a nice, polite boy."

"He's a big liar," Feep argued. "He lies all the time. Everybody hates him. And I saw him steal a jawbreaker at the candy store. At least Monkey would be an honest crook."

Mama sighed and gave up. "Put on a clean shirt before you leave the house," she told him.

Donna's mother came by while Grandma was still drying breakfast dishes, to borrow their electric iron.

"I know it's your ironing day, too," Mrs. Payne said, "but mine won't heat up and Alvin's wearing his last shirt today, and it's one that I turned the collar on."

Mama handed her the iron. "I'll come and get it after lunch. I wasn't in the mood to iron this morning, anyway. I got a copy of *Lost Horizon* at the library and I haven't even opened it yet, so I thought I'd curl up on the sofa and read."

Mrs. Payne eased herself into a chair and sighed. "My sister-in-law read it. She said she smiled all the way through, it made her so happy just thinking that there could be a magical place like that."

Grandma poured water from the steaming tea kettle into a cup and shook the tea ball in it. Then she set it in front of Mrs. Payne. "How's Donna coming along with her job?"

Mrs. Payne shook her head. "They sent her home early yesterday, but she didn't lose her enthusiasm. She left right on time this morning, more excited than I ever saw her before. I'm sorry she has to do this. I just wish she'd felt bad about it, too, so I'd have some faith that she'll go back to school some day. But we didn't know which way to turn. Alvin's mother is moving in with us, or did I already tell you that? She can't walk without help anymore, so I'll be the one taking care of her. And we've got to have a new roof before the real rainy season starts. That rain we had last night nearly filled up all the pans I put down."

"Donna is grown up for her age," Auntie Sis said. "She can handle this."

Quinn thought of saying that she was grown up, too. But she knew what Mama's response would be.

She left them talking over their morning tea, to watch Feep running down the block under the maple trees with his jacket pulled up over his head. The rain had stopped, but the trees still dripped. The last thing she heard from the women at the table was Mrs. Payne's question about Beau John. Had anyone heard from him?

Not yet. Not yet.

Quinn saw the mailman pass their house on his morning route while she was dusting the parlor windowsills. She saw him pass on his afternoon route while she pulled weeds from the soft damp earth in the rose bed.

Justin crossed the street while Quinn was washing her hands under the side yard faucet. He carried a basket of gooseberries, and held it awkwardly under one arm.

"Aunt Ramona said your grandmother knows how to make gooseberry dumplings," he said. "Here." He handed the basket to her. He blushed suddenly.

Quinn took the basket in her wet hands. "Thanks. Your aunts grow the best gooseberries in the neighborhood."

"Sure," he said. He looked around the yard, then at her. "Have you heard anything about your dad yet?"

Quinn started toward the back porch. "Not yet, but we will," she said. She wouldn't look back at him and hoped he'd go away, for fear he'd say something about Hooverville.

But he followed her instead. "Are you still going to work with Aunt Clotilde tomorrow? She's counting on you."

"I'll be there," Quinn said as she climbed the steps.

"Are you going to the movies tomorrow night?" Justin asked.

Quinn turned and stared at him. She had forgotten the Wednesday night movies.

"We always go," she said. "I guess we'll go this time, too."

Justin looked away, then back at her. "Then I'll see you there," he said. "Maybe we could sit together."

Quinn clutched the basket harder. What she had once wanted most was now happening, but she had forgotten this, too. "I usually sit with Donna," she stammered.

Justin swallowed visibly. "We could all sit together," he said.

Quinn nodded. "Yes, we could." Had she sounded too eager?

Justin whirled around and loped away. "See you later," he called out.

Mr. Shadwell, raking the Dallas cinder path, looked over and smiled at Quinn.

If Quinn could have captured the moment and kept it forever, she would have hurried to do so, even though this was no time for flirting with a boy. But the guilty pleasure was shattered a moment later when Elizabetta DePiano saw them and screamed one of her nearly unintelligible curses.

Quinn turned to stare. Elizabetta took one step toward her, then tottered off up the street again, wrapped in black, carrying her paper shopping bags. She began laughing, the laughter rising to a hysterical pitch. Then she swung around and jutted her chin toward Quinn.

"Where ees papa?" she cried. "Where ees?"

Goosebumps broke out on Quinn's arms.

She knows something, Quinn thought. That evil old woman knows something about Beau John.

Mr. Shadwell staggered down the cinder path, dragging his rake, one hand raised in a fist. Elizabetta cackled when she saw him and scurried on. Mr. Shadwell stopped and leaned on the rake. Quinn could see that he was breathing hard.

She hurried out the gate and ran across the road. "Are you all right?" she asked him.

His face was dark red. His mouth was trembling. When she reached him, he shook his head and turned away from her.

She touched his arm. "Let's go in the yard where you can sit down. Come on. You need to sit down for a while and so do I. She scares me."

Mr. Shadwell looked straight at her.

"She does," Quinn said. "I even wondered — for a moment — if she might know something about Beau John. Or if she found out something and told somebody."

Mr. Shadwell nodded slightly and then shrugged. He wondered, too.

But what could Elizabetta know about Beau John? He certainly wouldn't confide in her.

Miss Clotilde saw them coming through the gate and came out of the house to guide the old man to a chair on the porch. Quinn left again, and was walking toward her own gate when she saw Betty standing on her porch, dressed in a flimsy red and orange kimono, watching and smoking.

Quinn stood uncertainly in the middle of the road. Suddenly she remembered Feep telling Mama that

Monkey was an honest crook. Even when he was in trouble, he could be trusted.

Betty waved and Quinn waved back.

Betty, whose boyfriend Mike knew all sorts of people, had helped her once before.

Quinn walked across the street toward the young woman who waited for her.

Twelve

While Quinn climbed the steps, Betty watched old Mrs. DePiano scrabbling up the street.

"I hate her," Betty said in such a mild tone that Quinn burst out laughing without wanting to.

"She's awful," Quinn said.

Betty turned her gaze on Quinn then. Her eyes were like a painted doll's, bright blue and round. Even though she was not dressed, she wore heavy make-up and red glass earrings that dangled little chains and tarnished gold balls. "Sit down," she said.

Quinn perched nervously on the edge of a chipped bench, almost regretting the impulse that sent her across the street to talk to this young woman she barely knew, even though they had been neighbors for years.

Betty looked curiously at her. "Have you heard from Beau John yet?" she asked.

Quinn shook her head. "No. Not yet. I suppose Mike told you that I went to see him."

Betty grinned and inhaled smoke from her cigarette. "Sure, he told me. He said the boys down at the card room won't let him get over that very soon." She laughed. "A little kid with a braid sending somebody to the back room for him."

"I'm not a little kid," Quinn blurted.

"Sure, sure," Betty said.

"Mike told me to go talk to somebody called Double D who's staying in Hooverville. And I did."

Betty's penciled eyebrows rose in surprise. "No kidding," she said. "I wouldn't have gone anywhere near that place."

"You would if you were Beau John's daughter," Quinn said. "But I didn't get much help from Double D. They were stopped by the Federal police, but they got away. Double D is hurt. He doesn't know anything about my father."

Betty blinked. "Gee, kid, that's tough. It really is. Beau John's a nice man. He helped Mom get her insurance after Dad died. He went downtown and spoke up for her when the insurance company was trying to cheat her the way they always do."

Quinn hadn't known that. "Beau John likes to help people."

"Maybe he likes to help people too much," Betty said.

"What's that supposed to mean?"

Betty inhaled deeply and looked across the street at Quinn's house. "Maybe people who think more about themselves and less about other people get along better."

"You're making it sound as if my father meddled in other people's business and caused trouble," Quinn said.

Betty barked a quick laugh. "No, that's my mother you're talking about. Beau John doesn't meddle and judge. He just — I don't know. There's a difference. So you talked to this Double D guy and he couldn't help you?"

"No, he couldn't, but maybe I understand a little more about what Beau John's been doing," Quinn said.

Betty shook her head. "He shouldn't have mixed himself up with those guys. He should have left it to the men who do things like that all the time. Of course, nobody could trust *them* with so much money. The big boys knew Beau John was out of work and having hard times, but they still trusted him. Don't that beat all?"

Quinn looked down at the splintered porch floor. Abruptly, she asked, "What does old Elizabetta know about my father?"

Betty's face turned red and she blinked furiously. "What makes you think she knows anything?"

"Because of things she says. I got to thinking about how your mother started going back to church with the DePianos . . ."

"And she sent the priest around to see me," Betty said disgustedly. "As if that could change my mind."

"The old woman hates gangsters because her son in Chicago was killed by them. So I guess she hates Mike, too. I guess she'd take your mother's side against Mike, wouldn't she?"

Betty's face was so red it looked as if it must hurt. "Well, that won't last much longer. Mike and I are getting married pretty soon. Then I won't have to listen to them anymore."

Quinn didn't say anything. The silence drew out. Somewhere someone was pounding on wood, thump, thump, thump, and then a child began shrieking suddenly.

"Is that your brother?" Betty asked.

"No, that's Monkey," Quinn said. "They're building an airplane."

"Kids," Betty said.

"Did you ever tell your mother that Beau John was doing things like Mike does, and he's still nice?" Quinn asked suddenly. "I think I might have."

Betty's hand trembled a little, then stopped. She dropped her cigarette on the porch floor and ground it out with her scuffed red satin slippers.

When Betty didn't answer, Quinn said, "I'd have said that to her because it's true. My father is a good person, no matter what. Your mother knows that."

Betty examined her red nail polish. "She knows."

"So did she try to defend you and tell Elizabetta that?"

Betty's smile was twisted. "Who knows what she said?"

"But she told Elizabetta."

Betty shrugged.

Quinn sighed. "That's what Elizabetta is always yelling about, then. She told somebody about my father, and she's laughing because Beau John didn't come home."

Betty pulled a gold cigarette case out of the pocket in her kimono, found a cigarette, and lit it with a gold lighter. "I don't know. It's possible. She told the Seattle police about Mike, but his uncle fixed things with them."

Quinn looked down at her feet. "I heard a man say that nobody can fix things with the Federal police."

"That's what Mike says."

Tears ran straight down Quinn's face suddenly. "Do you know what's going to happen?"

"Mike says that Prohibition will be over pretty soon. Liquor will be legal. He says the bootleggers will be out of business, and all the smart guys have already dropped out. He says when the law changes, nobody who used to be involved in smuggling will go to jail." She laughed a little. "There aren't enough jails to hold them."

Quinn raised her head. "Does that mean that if Beau

John can hide long enough, people will stop looking for him?"

Betty shrugged. "Sounds like it to me."

"You could ask Mike again."

Betty shook her head. "Not a chance," she said. "He doesn't like questions."

"But if you hear something?"

Betty studied the end of her cigarette. "If I hear something, and if I'm still here, I'll make sure you find out."

"Thanks," Quinn breathed. Now she couldn't stop smiling. "Thanks."

"Sure, kiddo." Betty was about to turn away, but she scowled and said, "Darn that old man! There he is again."

Quinn turned and saw Mr. Shadwell, raking the cinder path again.

"You don't need to worry about him," Quinn said. "If he knows anything about anybody, he'll never tell." The words were out of her mouth before she realized it, and Betty flushed.

"He watches me and Mike."

"Maybe he's worried about you, like everybody else," Quinn said as kindly as possible.

Betty tossed her dry curls. "I saw Amy's boyfriend drive up in his big car last Sunday," she said. "He looks like some kind of fussy little *clerk*."

The spite shocked Quinn, but she didn't dare retaliate, even if she had known how. She walked down the steps, looked back, and then said, "Take care of yourself, Betty."

Betty hesitated a moment, and then said, "You, too, kid."

When she walked in her own house, Auntie Sis said, "Mercy, what were you doing across the street?"

Quinn shrugged as casually as she could. "She waved at me so I walked over. She says she and Mike will be getting married pretty soon. It made me think of Amy."

"I hope you didn't say anything to her about Amy!" Mama exclaimed. "We wouldn't want the neighborhood talking about your sister until we're sure what's going to happen."

"I didn't say anything, but Betty saw Carl drive up Sunday."

"Oh, well, that can't hurt," Mama said, satisfied. "I wish we'd hear from your father so we can make a few plans. I'm sure Carl expects to meet him soon."

"He's working hard, Mom," Quinn said. She brushed past her mother and ran upstairs.

Where are you, Beau John?

Feep and Monkey distinguished themselves the following day by hauling their wood-and-brown-paper airplane up on Monkey's back porch roof, launching it, and crashing it into the dahlia bed prized by Monkey's father. Both were hurt, but neither of them seriously. The dahlias were destroyed.

"Why do you do things like this?" Grandma demanded of Feep as she poured peroxide on his cuts and scrapes while Quinn tried to hold him still. "Why do you scare your mother half to death when your father isn't home and Dick's out looking for a job, and there's nobody around to smack the tar out of you?"

"Don't you smack me!" Feep cried, trying to squirm away from Quinn.

"Somebody ought to," Quinn muttered. Her mother and Auntie Sis had gone to the store first thing after breakfast, taking almost all of the last of the money, and they would be horrified at the escapade when they heard about it. Things were bad enough already. But they wouldn't give Feep what Quinn thought he deserved.

"Let Beau John smack me!" Feep insisted.

Hopeless. Beau John had never spanked anybody.

After Feep's injuries had been taken care of, Quinn ran across the street to begin work with Miss Clotilde. They sat inside that day, because a hard wind was blowing dust and pollen around the back yard.

"Mr. Shadwell is sick this morning," Miss Clotilde observed as she lettered a careful capital *M* on an envelope.

"What's wrong with him?" Quinn asked, looking up.

"I think he's just wearing out," Miss Clotilde said. "He's older than the hills."

"He's even older than we are," Miss Ramona cackled. She sliced tomatoes for the sandwiches they would eat at lunch. Lettuce soaked in cold water in the sink.

Justin came in, letting the screen door slam behind him. He held a yellow apple in each hand. "What do you think?" he asked his aunts. "Are they ripe enough?"

Each woman took an apple and examined it carefully. "They're ripe, all right," Miss Ramona said. "Do you think you can fill a couple of boxes by this afternoon? We need the money, and Dick can take them down to the market."

"He won't be back until dinnertime," Quinn said, head bent over her work.

"Tomorrow morning will have to be soon enough," Justin said. "There are more coming along behind these, but I don't think they'll be ready until close to the end of the month. And then there's the tree in back that won't be ready until September."

"We'll keep those for ourselves, just as we always do," Miss Clotilde said absently.

"Mr. Shadwell might not be up to making cider this year," Miss Ramona said. "Grinding up those apples is hard work."

"We can do it, sister," Miss Clotilde said as she

dipped a pen point in India ink. She laughed and shook her head. "Nice hard cider for the cold weather. Doesn't it sound delicious?"

She got Quinn's attention. "You have hard cider? I thought it was illegal."

"Oh, bosh," Miss Clotilde said. "Not if we make it ourselves. I think it's only illegal if we sell it."

"No, no, it's illegal to have it," Miss Ramona said.

"Is that so? Are you sure?" Miss Clotilde put down her pen. "Why, now, I never heard that."

"Well, maybe I'm wrong," Miss Ramona said. "I never could keep all that Prohibition business straight, and it didn't seem to matter much to anybody."

Miss Clotilde picked up her pen again. "It makes no nevermind, sister. According to the papers these last weeks, the law's going to be changed any day now and that's that. We'll be able to make cider that's hard enough to knock our hats off."

Justin, pouring a glass of water for himself, laughed. "Oh, that's going to make my mother happy," he said. "She'd love to see your hats knocked off at Thanksgiving dinner."

"Ours and everybody else's," Miss Ramona said serenely as she went on slicing tomatoes. "I never noticed anybody turning our cider down."

Quinn was having trouble concentrating. "What do the newspapers say about Prohibition?" she asked.

"Why, only that it's almost over," Miss Clotilde said. "How many invitations have you done? You're a hard worker, Quinn. When you're older, I'm going to talk to the manager of the stationery department about you. I think you'd be a perfect employee for them. Goodness knows you know more about pens and paper than she does."

Quinn looked up. "Really?" She'd never given a serious thought to a job.

"Certainly. How far along are you in high school now?"

"I'll be a sophomore this year," Quinn said.

"Three years until you graduate," Miss Clotilde said slowly, tapping the end of her pen against her chin. "Well, the store will still be there," she concluded briskly, going back to work. "No hurry."

But Quinn was dazzled. She could quit school now. She could get a job. She would take her rightful position with the women in the family.

She could take Beau John's place until he came home.

Except that Mama would never let her.

"Quinn, is your family going to the movie tonight?" Miss Ramona asked as she dried her hands.

"I think so," Quinn said. She looked sideways at Justin and saw that he was blushing again. She grinned to herself.

"I wondered if they would," Miss Ramona said. "I remember your grandma saying if she ever won new dishes, she'd never go back because the movies give her such a headache."

"I don't think she'd stay home," Quinn said doubtfully. "Well, maybe. But she'd like to win groceries, too."

"Who wouldn't?" Miss Ramona said. "Who wouldn't?"

Quinn returned to her work. Was there ever a time when people didn't hope they'd win things by buying a five-cent ticket to the Wednesday night movies? Beau John said there had been, and there would be again.

"Good times are coming," he'd told her a hundred times. "They're lining up for us, like magic boxes along that path to the top of the hill. We'll open them one by one, and when we get to the top, we'll find the pot of gold, daughter."

When Quinn left after lunch that day, Justin said, "See you tonight, Quinn." Then he lowered his voice and said, "I hope you hear from your dad today."

Quinn only nodded and hurried home.

But the only mail that came was a bill from Auntie Sis's dentist, insisting on a partial payment on the four-dollar bill.

Uncle Dick came home five minutes before dinner,

pleased that he'd found a half-day's work, with the promise of another half-day the following week.

"I'm paying for the movie tonight, folks," he announced. "I'm a rich man." He dropped a handful of change into the cigar box and looked around, smiling. "Wait until Beau John gets here. He'll fill the cigar box up to the top."

Thirteen

During dinner, the sky clouded over and the wind dropped off. By the time Grandma and Auntie Sis had washed and wiped the last of the pots and pans, a light mist was falling.

"Won't last," Uncle Dick predicted, standing in the open kitchen doorway with his hands in his pockets, rocking back and forth a little. "No need to worry, ladies. You won't need your umbrellas tonight."

"You've never guessed right about the weather yet," Grandma said as she tipped water out of the dishpan. "If it keeps on raining, I'm staying home."

"You can't," Auntie Sis objected. "I heard from two different people that there'll be five dollars cash in one of the grocery bags tonight. We'll need all the tickets we can get."

"My word," Uncle Dick marveled. "It would be worth going out and coming back in a couple of times to get the extra tickets."

"Let's do that, Uncle Dick," Feep said.

"No, no, they'll be watching for cheaters," Auntie Sis said. She dried the dishpan and put it under the sink.

Amy looked around at her family, clearly disappointed. "I planned to stay home tonight, but now I guess I can't."

Quinn stared at her. "You never miss Wednesday nights."

"I know, but I bought a card of bobby pins today, and I wanted to try out pincurls tonight. One of the women in the office showed me how. It'll be too late to wash my hair when we get home."

"Better wait until early Sunday," Mama said. "That way, if your hair doesn't turn out right you still have time to wet it down and start over."

"You could think about getting a permanent wave," Quinn said. "There was a girl in school last year who had one."

"Is she the one you told us about before?" Mama asked. "The one whose hair caught fire?"

"No, Mama," Amy said. "You're thinking about Gerry Peal, remember?"

"No I'm not, dearie," Mama said. "It wasn't Gerry Peal who had the permanent wave. It was her aunt from Michigan who went in a shop to get one but the wires electrocuted her. I don't trust those machines."

"Donna's cousin gets permanent waves all the time," Quinn said.

"Then why are they called 'permanent'?" Uncle Dick asked.

All the women looked sharply at him to see if he was teasing them, but his expression was perfectly sober. Before anyone could answer, Donna came through the open door behind him.

"I'm early, but I need to talk to Quinn for a minute," she said.

Quinn was pleased. Donna often came early and waited in Quinn's bedroom while she got ready for the movie. She would not have been surprised if her friend stopped the practice, since she had changed her life so abruptly. But here she was, the same old Donna.

"When's your grandma coming to stay?" Auntie Sis asked Donna.

"Not until Saturday," Donna told her as she followed Quinn to the stairs. "After this week, Mama might not be going to go to Grocery Night because Grandma's pretty sick."

Upstairs, Quinn closed her bedroom door to keep Feep out. "How was work today?" she asked Donna.

"Fine, I guess," Donna said. She sat on Quinn's bed and kicked off her shoes. "But I'm so tired. I'll get used to it, though. Amy did."

Quinn changed to a freshly ironed cotton dress and tied a matching ribbon on her braid. "Amy's feet hurt a lot."

"So do mine. I never get to sit down."

Quinn checked her appearance in her mirror, then snatched up her jacket. "Did you bring an umbrella?"

"I left it on the porch."

Quinn, who had her hand on the doorknob, turned back. "How can Justin walk with us if we all have umbrellas?"

"Boys never carry umbrellas."

"Will he walk under one of ours?" Quinn asked.

Donna shook her head slowly. "I don't know. I suppose he'll walk under yours. But I don't think there's room for three of us on the sidewalk if two of us carry umbrellas."

"You're right," Quinn said, dismayed. "This isn't going to work. I can't walk with him alone. I wouldn't know what to talk about."

"Aren't you ever alone with him at the cottage? Out in the yard? In the orchard?"

"Heavens, no," Quinn said. "There's always somebody around, talking, so I don't have to think up things. It's a long way to the movie house. What am I going to say?"

"Maybe he won't really want to walk with us," Donna said. "Maybe he only meant to sit with us after we get there. Then you don't need to talk."

"It's all so complicated!" Quinn exclaimed.

"Ask your sister what to do after this. She must be able to work all this out, because she has a boyfriend."

"She thinks I'm a baby."

Feep screamed her name from downstairs, so Quinn opened the door. "We'd better go," she told Donna.

"Smile," Donna said. "Justin might be waiting downstairs."

Quinn's mouth went dry.

Justin waited on the porch for them, with his jacket collar turned up and a light mist of rain on his hair.

"My aunts already left," he told Mama. "But they're slow. You could catch up."

"Oh, let's do," Mama said as she opened her umbrella. "It's always so nice to walk with friends. Get under here with me, Grandma, and let Sis and Dick use your umbrella. It's better than theirs. Is everybody ready?"

Feep tore away, his raincoat flapping, to join Monkey, who had been waiting across the street. Quinn watched in agony as her family paired up and hurried to walk with the Dallas sisters.

Justin seemed oblivious to the awkward moment that followed when he, Donna, and Quinn hesitated at the gate.

"Donna, walk with me," Amy called out suddenly. "I want to ask you something." She waited at the corner, smiling out from under her umbrella at them.

Donna hesitated, then closed her umbrella and

ducked under Amy's. Amy nodded at Quinn before walking away.

Quinn's first impulse was to turn and run back inside the house. What could she say to Justin that he wouldn't think was stupid and boring?

"Come on," he said. "They're getting ahead of us. Gosh, the rain's really coming down hard now. Let me hold your umbrella higher, so I can get under it with you."

Rain drummed on the umbrella and ran off it in sheets while they crossed the street. The others were half a block ahead, and no one looked back.

"I like rain," Justin said with satisfaction.

They were enclosed in a small and private world, with the rain cutting them off from interruption or distraction. Quinn looked up into Justin's eyes.

"Quinn," he said softly. "Gosh." And he smiled.

The theater was always crowded on Wednesdays, but that night all the seats were filled. Quinn and Justin, unable to find places in the same row with Quinn's family, sat behind them with Donna's parents and the Kirks, whose baby girl surprised them by falling asleep before the curtain went up.

"If I'm lucky, I won't have to go upstairs and sit in the crying room this time," Mrs. Kirk whispered to Quinn. The crying room was a small, comfortable place behind a soundproof glass window, next to the women's restroom.

Grandma, sitting in front of Quinn, turned around to ask her if she had her ticket stub. Quinn held it up.

"Put it in your pocket so you don't lose it," Grandma said. "You, too, Justin. I've got a good feeling about tonight."

Quinn grinned. And then she remembered when Grandma had told her that she had a feeling Beau John wasn't coming home last weekend.

Beau John.

How could she have forgotten her father?

She leaned away from Justin, as if it was his fault that she had become so dazzled by his eyes that she forgot.

The movie began, a comedy they all wanted to see, and Quinn tried to force herself to concentrate.

Halfway through, she became aware of a stir in the row she sat in. Mrs. Kirk, next to her, leaned toward her and whispered, "Betty's asking for you."

Quinn leaned forward and saw the circle of light from Betty's flashlight shining on the carpet at the end of her row.

"What?" someone whispered. "Who? Who?"

"She wants you, Quinn," Mrs. Kirk whispered.

Quinn got up and stepped over all the feet between her seat and the aisle, wondering, half-frightened and half-resentful. What could Betty want? Had Grandma or Mama noticed what was going on?

When she reached the aisle, Betty whispered, "Come out to the lobby right now."

Quinn followed her up the aisle and through the velvet curtains. "What's going on?" she asked Betty.

"Somebody's looking for you," Betty said. She was angry. Her cheeks flamed and her doll eyes glinted.

"Who?" Quinn asked, mystified. There was no one in the lobby.

Betty handed Quinn a wet scrap of paper with her name on it, printed in block letters. "That old man is waiting for you outside," she said.

Quinn stared at her. "I don't know who you're talking about."

"Mr. Shadwell," Betty hissed. "He bought a ticket, but all he did was wander up and down the aisles until he spotted you. And then he gave me this piece of paper and went outside. He's waiting by the ticket booth."

Why would Mr. Shadwell want to call her out of the theater? Quinn hesitated a moment, wondering if she should find the Dallas sisters and take them with her. Or Justin.

Betty disappeared through the velvet curtains, leaving Quinn to solve the problem. Quinn bit her lip, shrugged, and went through the exit door.

Mr. Shadwell stood outside the glow of the theater signs, wet and shivering in the doorway of the closed hat shop next door. When he saw her, he moved forward a step.

"What are you doing here?" Quinn asked as she joined him.

He held his hand up, measuring space, and pointed to Quinn.

"Beau John!" she exclaimed.

Mr. Shadwell held a gnarled finger to his lips.

"You've seen him?" Quinn whispered.

He nodded.

"Where?"

Mr. Shadwell turned and pointed toward the corner, and made a gesture as if shooing her in that direction.

Quinn took off running, and a dark figure stepped forward from another doorway.

"You're back!" Quinn cried as she reached for her father. "You're back!"

Beau John hugged her hard enough to keep her from breathing for a moment. "I knew you'd all be here tonight," he said. "Lucky for me, I found Mr. Shadwell home and he was willing to try to get you outside so I could see you."

"Are you all right? You aren't hurt or sick?"

"I'm fine. But how's your mother? Tell me the truth."

"She had a bad spell one day, but she got over it. Let me go get the others! They won't care about winning anything if they know you're home."

"No, no," Beau John said. "I can't stay. And I don't want them to know I was here."

Quinn backed up a step. "Why? We've been so worried. Uncle Dick said you probably found a way to earn more money, but I . . . but I . . ."

"But you knew better," Beau John said. He hugged her again. "You were always the one I feared would find out. But listen to me, daughter. Don't ever go to Hooverville again. Most of the men are good, but Mr. Shadwell can't protect you from the ones who aren't."

"How did you find out I'd been there?"

"I heard it on the hobo telegraph, but nobody knew how you'd found out anything to start with."

Quinn leaned her cheek against her father's wet coat. "I overheard you talking to that awful man who came to the house . . ."

"That was Johnny," Beau John said bitterly. "I didn't want him to come."

"And then Betty Caster said something about you and Mike knowing the same people."

"Did you find out about Double D from Mike?"

Quinn nodded. "I went to the card room . . ."

Beau John laughed a little. "I bet the boys never got over that."

"Why can't you come home now? Didn't you give back the money?"

"Every cent. I couldn't take chances moving around until I returned it. But I can't stay here."

"The Federal police are looking for you, aren't they?" Quinn asked.

"Did they come to the house?" he asked quickly.

Quinn shook her head.

Beau John sighed and leaned his face against the top of her head. "I prayed they wouldn't bother. I'm not worth chasing, not like some, but they might keep me if they found me again. Somebody made it easy for them the first time. I had a hunch I was being followed after I crossed over the bridge when I left here the last time, but I couldn't be sure."

"Did Elizabetta DePiano turn you in?"

"I don't know. Maybe."

"Can't you come home with us tonight?" Quinn begged. "Just one night before you leave again?"

"I can't take the risk of someone seeing me, and it's breaking my heart. I've already mailed the letter that will explain how I found this good job in Canada. And it's true, daughter. A job is waiting for me. As soon as I can, I'll send for your mother to come and visit. And before you know it, the laws will change and I'll be in the clear and back home again."

"Mama will be so hurt that you didn't call her out of the theater."

"She's not the one who went looking for me in that hell-hole under the bridge." He kissed her forehead. "Promise you won't look for me again. I'll come home as soon as I can. Don't tell them you've seen me — they'll only worry."

"But *I'll* worry," Quinn said.

"You have to be strong enough bear it all alone," her father said. "That's the hardest kind of worry. Tomorrow, when my letter gets to the house, you'll have an address where you can write me. Tell me everything, good and bad, because you know your mother won't. I'll be watching the news in the Canadian papers, and when it's safe, I'll come home. It can't be more than a few weeks or months now."

"And nobody will be looking for smugglers after the law changes?"

"They'll keep looking for the big ones." He laughed a little. "I've never been much of a success, daughter, not even at smuggling."

She wept as she hugged him hard. "You *are* a success. You are, Dad."

Dad. The word hung between them. She had never called him that before.

He held her out at arm's length and studied her face. It took a moment for both of them to understand what had happened, what she had lost with her childhood's trust. His eyes filled with tears and he shook his head.

"What have I done?" he asked.

"Nothing! Nothing! You always tried the best you could." But he was her father, human and imperfect, not Beau John who had always been better than perfect in her eyes.

Neither of them spoke for a long moment. Then he

said, "I've got to go. Someone's waiting in a car around the corner. Write to me!"

"I will, I promise."

He bent and kissed her forehead. "Little girl, I'm so sorry."

And then he pulled away from her and was gone into the rain and darkness.

She raised her hand to wave, but he didn't look back. And she couldn't call out the name that would have made him look back. The magic was gone.

Mr. Shadwell touched her arm. When she turned, he pointed to the theater.

"I'll go back in," she said. "Thank you for helping us. You watched out for us, didn't you?" She reached for his hand and squeezed it. "Everything's going to be fine now. Go home and get into dry clothes. I'll come by to see you tomorrow and make sure you're all right. I'll tell you all about the movie and who won the prizes."

Mr. Shadwell raised his free hand high, measuring space, and lowered it slowly until it reached Quinn's head. Then he pointed at her.

She knew what he meant. She was Beau John's daughter. The smuggler's daughter. The storyteller's daughter.

She took off her jacket in the lobby and bundled it under her arm. Betty ignored her. When Quinn found her seat in the dark, Justin whispered, "Where were you?"

"Talking to Betty."

"Why?"

"Hush, I want to watch the movie." She stared blindly at the screen, blinking back tears and aching all over as if she had fallen from a great height.

Justin reached out and touched her braid. "You've been outside," he whispered. "Your hair's wet."

"It's so stuffy in here."

"You left your umbrella under your seat."

"Hush."

He waited a moment, then leaned close to her. "Is everything all right?"

"Yes."

"I mean, is *everything* all right?"

"I think so." With her free hand, she wiped away a tear that streaked down her face.

He reached out his hand and she took it, and felt herself smiling. He held her hand tightly until the lights went up and the theater manager walked out on the stage.

"Tonight's a lucky night for somebody," he called out.

Justin looked over at Quinn. "He's right, isn't he?" he asked.

She nodded.

Justin dug through his shirt pocket and pulled out

his ticket stub. "Here," he said as he handed it to Quinn. "If you're on a lucky streak, take this. If you win groceries, maybe I could come over for lunch. I'm getting sick of tuna fish."

"You could come over even if I don't win," Quinn said.

"Sure," Justin said.

Quinn slid down in her seat and hugged herself. "Sure," she said.